MARK RAMSDEN has played saxophone in a wide variety of professional contexts; chiefly jazz-related, although also with countless show-business luminaries, including Tom Robinson (hit single 'War Baby'). He has also been a rather speculative psychic and astrologer and the editor of cutting-edge sex magazine *Fetish Times*. His serious music occasionally surfaces on Radio 3 and his pierced and weighted genitalia appear far too often in magazines and on television. A sober alcoholic with a taste for hallucinogenics, he lives in London with his partner, their son and a discarnate entity called Lola.

The
DARK MAGUS
and the
SACRED WHORE

Mark Ramsden

Library of Congress Catalog Card Number: 98–86411

A catalogue record for this book is available from
the British Library on request

The right of Mark Ramsden to be identified as the author
of this work has been asserted by him in accordance with the
Copyright, Designs and Patents Act 1988

First published by Serpent's Tail,
4 Blackstock Mews, London N4

Website: www.serpentstail.com

Phototypeset in Caslon by Intype London Ltd
Printed in Great Britain by Mackays of Chatham, plc

10 9 8 7 6 5 4 3 2 1

For Bobbie, the best moll ever
and for
Dagmar and Raphael, the sunshine people

Contents

1

Good
Friday

'YES! YES! HARDER, you little vixen!'

The baby monitor at my side crackles with the familiar tones of Rob Powers, the sort of fifty-year-old rock star who has a leather face to go with the trousers. And before you start, this is not a fictional Lou Reed. The real Rob Powers is even less good at singing, dancing or making people happy. He has an even shakier relationship with the tempered scale than that croaking old cackpiece. I tried hard to fit in the word charlatan somewhere, but it ceased to be an insult round about the time Andy Warhol legitimised both their careers.

Fame has bought Rob homes in many countries, good-looking women and sulky-looking boys, some painful divorce settlements, expensive delirium, even more expensive cures, renowned shrinks, more wives, children, shrinks for his children and maybe even shrinks for the shrinks by now. He has bought everything money can buy except happiness, I'm glad to say. Which is why he comes to me, or more accurately to my live-in deity Sasha Kristinson, a woman who manages to channel the awesome powers of the goddess Kali despite being five foot two inches tall. She doesn't use blue face make-up or wear a string of skulls round her neck, least not round the house, but one bolt of lightning from those shimmering turquoise eyes and you know you are in the presence.

'Don't you just hate being a personal therapy consultant?' I say to Nails, who is trying to concentrate on our chess game. 'I mean, even in management it's just not a prestigious career.'

Nails grunts, which I take as further encouragement to share.

'It's a little bit like being a plumber in that we provide essential services but everyone hates us.'

Nails holds a bejewelled black hand up to stem the flow of verbiage, so I content myself with priming the espresso machine, which requires some especially distracting rattling and clanking. I picture Sasha as I do so, her crown of blonde thorns as teased and tormented as our twisted clientele. If Rob is blindfolded she will be wearing fluffy pink carpet slippers with her shiny black rubber stuff. It helps her to know that the customers are not getting what they paid for, an English trait she must have picked up from me.

The baby monitor crackles with another message from Planet Rob.

'You're going to pay for this one day, you bitch! You're going to roast in hell! Aaargh! Wooagh!'

All of which sounds strangely similar to the hate mail she gets from the moral majority. Sasha also manifests as a bewildering number of minor goddesses on the performance art circuit, although whether the original deities would have fitted quite so much fruit up their fundamental orifices is open to question. She calls it exploring the interface between sex, religion, art and nature. The police tend to call it something else, especially the further you get from the Lower East Side. Whenever the gigs dry up she ministers to the sick, which is what is going on next door.

'You filthy whore, you dirty, dirty, festering . . . Wurgh! Aaah!'

Rob lapses into glossalia again while I wonder whether he has ever talked so long without mentioning New York City. Indeed, if you took the two words New York out of any of Rob's songs and replaced them with the word Cleethorpes, his many deficiencies as a songwriter would become clear to the vast army of lobotomised sheep who worship him. But don't let me put you off him. Let him speak for himself.

'Not the grater! No! Please! No! No! YES!! No!'

Rob has his ego blown up to barrage-balloon size every time he goes to work by a team of skilful sycophants. But every time Sasha gives him his orders he is only too happy to dance to her tune. He likes to carp and whine as he does so, but then he did start off as a protest singer.

'Let me go! Come on, that's enough now!'

A bloodcurdling screech causes my guest Nails to look up from the chessboard where he has been trying to unravel an opening I looked up in a book beforehand. It's the Dragon variation of the Ruy Lopez if you want to bond with us.

Appropriately enough, Nails is playing black. Even more appropriately, I am playing white. A white Englishman is even whiter than a white American Protestant in New York, but it does not take long for people to peg me as Eurotrash. We, the English, are not always welcome here, just like everywhere else, come to think of it. Even the asshole formerly known as Prince Charles wouldn't draw much of a crowd now his meal ticket has gone to meet her dressmaker. Which would be the position I would find myself in in New York if Sasha and I ever split.

'You will pay for this, you evil bitch!' says Rob, rather unwisely I would have thought. Sasha gives him another prod with whatever trident she is using presently, and the screaming starts again. By my side is a life-size replica of the demon Pazazu, the scaly winged terror of ancient Babylon who recently tried to make a comeback in the movie *The Exorcist*. I haven't heard much of him recently, but maybe like a lot of people in show business he got bitter and took to drink. Sasha brought him home yesterday and I just hope he's house-trained. I pat him on the head occasionally to remind Nails that although he might be wearing pointy mauve crocodile shoes I have Satan and his host of demons on my side.

'No! No! NO! NO! NONONO!'

There is a lot of screaming at this point. More than the director of a splatter flick would find appropriate. More than even Yoko Ono or Diamanda Galas would dare to inflict on their small but select public.

At this point Nails loses some of his cool and shifts uneasily in his seat. He looks immaculate, as ever, but I happen to know that he once wore a stunning iridescent orange suit that didn't match the yellow Ferrari he was driving that day. It was the only sartorial lapse I can remember him making, but I haven't forgiven him yet. And I will never forget.

Nails spends a lot on his clothes, the sort of brightly coloured plumage that black personal therapy consultants always seem to wear in order to help the police identify them. Today he is wearing clean, expensive sports clothes which carry prominent brand names. The reds of his eyes advertise Rémy Martin brandy, and the inelegant sniffs with which he is hoping to repair his shredded sinuses are a just-say-no advert for cocaine. His hair is about two centimetres long and has improbable whorls and swoops shaved into it.

'Neat shoes, man,' says Nails, looking at my new shiny red

Doctor Martens. 'You got a lot of those boots, right? You starting some sort of skinhead gang?'

'You'd never know I was a teenage hippie, would you?'

'You'd know.' There is some irritating chuckling here that I can't let pass.

'Still too scared to get any piercings?' I say. 'Or a proper tattoo? Or a brand or a scarification?'

'White boy stuff,' he says. 'Don't need it.'

'You're just too chicken to let someone push a needle right through your dick and then attach a ring to it,' I say and then watch him blanch.

But one tussle he will always win hands down is being blacker than I am, and because he knows it gets on my tits he has bought a copy of *The Final Call* and placed it next to the board. Remembering that Nails was just a mere hour late for our chess game inspires me to challenge *The Final Call's* apocalyptic headline.

'When this conflict between the forces of good and evil breaks out, Nails, you know why the infidel is going to triumph?' I say.

He couldn't care less but I tell him anyway.

'Our army is just going to show up on time. And when you lot arrive, stoned and three days late, we will already have won.'

He ignores me while Rob says something that no one would ever print.

Nails shifts in his seat uneasily. He is surprisingly puritanical when it comes to the cutting edge of the personal therapy business. As the howls of our tormented client continue to crackle through the baby monitor Nails is twitchy. It's not often he leaves me even a chink in his armour, so I have to go with this one.

'That's a real cheese grater,' I say. 'She's using it just where you think she is.'

Nails's legs jackknife shut as I pick up one of my bishops and insert it in a handy pencil sharpener. I watch him flinch as I pretend to sharpen the end of it.

'You're weird, man,' says Nails, his voice hushed.

'Weird? You've got an anthropology degree, right? You never come across these initiation rituals before?'

'You do an initiation once,' he says. 'He does that . . . once a week?'

'He once took three exes, real ones if you can imagine such a thing, and stayed in the studio for a twenty-four-hour session. By the time he came out he looked like Bob Hope's scrotum. Your move.'

But Nails is still stalled, probably still pondering on that cheese grater.

'No! You wouldn't! You promised! You little bitch!' continues Rob, and I hope you will forgive the informality but I feel I know him well enough, having listened to every one of these sessions for a year now.

We have it on tape too, but I just can't interest the major companies in signing him up right now. It's a shame because he's between deals at the moment and something like this could really shift some units. It's certainly heartfelt. Gut-wrenchingly sincere. Real soul music.

'Aaargh! Waaagh! Wooaah! Do it again! Now! Right now!'

Suddenly Sasha's ice-cool faux-Chelsea drawl breaks through. She is from Michigan, but she knows domination sounds better in an English accent, bless her. 'Be silent, you loathsome wretch!'

Nails sits up straighter in his seat. It seems colder all of a sudden.

'How dare you foul the air of this sacred space with your inane slaverings!'

Nails probably needs subtitles by now as his women do not

feel themselves possessed by ancient deities. Not during working hours, anyway.

'She's on her goddess trip again,' I say, helpful as ever, although I'm never quite sure where the boundaries between being a sex therapist/goddess/performance artist/loving housewife and chocolate fiend begin and end. I don't think Sasha knows either.

The left side of Nails's mouth puckers just about as much as a gnat's asshole struggling to contain a social indiscretion. In his world whores are not modern-day manifestations of Aphrodite. They are there to worship him, not the other way round. But that's enough feeling superior to Nails. Sasha and I owe him money, and he might be here to kill us for all I know. Which is another reason to win this game of chess. Might as well go out on a high.

'Sash got any money right now?' says Nails.

'Ask her,' I say. 'And you know it's Sasha with an A.'

We are on very dangerous ground here. I'm going to have calluses on my little finger typing that extra A so often, but she would turn me into a toad if I were ever to use the diminutive. It's a short person thing, I think.

'She should dump you and marry him,' he says, voicing one of my deepest fears.

Sasha, with an A and don't you forget it, has already married one American rock star. She may even have killed him but we will get to that later. I keep telling her to kill Rob, but she just wags a reproving finger at me and sends me to the bank with our money. Well, I earn it too. You try listening to this stuff and greeting the clients. And make the coffee, send out for bagels and occasionally resuscitate those who should have consulted their doctors before they entered the temple of doom. We very nearly lost Rob once when we left him unattended for half an hour. When we unzipped him his rubber catsuit was full of puke, an experience which hasn't found its way into one of his songs as yet.

Like many another, including me, he tends to dwell on other people's deficiencies in his work. The bloodcurdling screeches turn into an uneasy rumble coming from the back of Rob's throat, something like the noise polecats make when they make love. Sometimes it sounds like he's saying something, but you can't quite make out the words, just like his live performances, come to think of it . . . I'll try not to go on. I don't like Rob much. Let's leave it at that.

'Decisions, decisions,' I say, but Nails is not going to make a move just yet. I get up and walk to the window from where I can see a rusted Lower East Side fire escape, some trash cans and some drying washing. A glance at the floor tells me the Roach Motel has another visitor. Some little turd in an anorak is singing soundlessly on the television while we listen to Bill Evans playing Cole Porter on the sound system. In England this stuff used to make me think of silver cocktail shakers, nights on Broadway, breakfast at Tiffany's and also misery, pain and then posthumous acclaim – the full jazz package. Now I am actually here I would give anything to be back in South London, bored to death and dreaming of somewhere exotic, but you probably know all that. We all do it.

Even when Sasha and I are at it – sorry, making love, or perhaps doing the nasty as they say here – I'm usually invoking the usual pantheon of obliging gods and goddesses who respond to every single cerebral twitch instantly and without heed for their own private agendas. They'll do *anything*.

As Rob screeches on I think about turning the music up but then I might not hear when he puts his saggy grey hands around Sasha's neck and squeezes till something snaps. Not that Rob is likely to break the habit of a lifetime and do something interesting, but he just might. He is not a well man.

I look at the photobooth portraits of me and Sasha, tacked up on the noticeboard where we write icky little messages to each other. We had some pictures done the day we met, by which time we already knew it was going to be special, and we have one done every anniversary. There are four strips now. In too many of these pictures I'm looking at her and she's looking at the camera, but then she has always been the sort of person who could be drowned by leaving a mirror at the bottom of a swimming-pool.

'So how's your Satanic scam going?' says Nails, having made his move, a feeble thrust which I parry with ease.

'Scam? The Black Church of Eternal Hellfire is not a scam.'

'You're still not as rich as L. Ron Hubbard.'

This is true, but as I only started the whole thing to settle a bet with Sasha I'm not doing too badly. With just a couple of small ads and an Internet site I managed to hook enough customers to start a small select coven. I have since lifted several curses at two thousand dollars each, and each ticket to my infernal cheese and wine parties costs five thousand dollars. It's not in Sasha's league. Yet. But she thinks I should invest and expand my client base. I suppose that's why she bought the little demon – it might even be tax deductible, come to think of it.

'You know this is how the fallen angel started in the first place,' Sasha said at the time. 'Jealousy. He wanted to prove he was better than God.'

'Which makes you the goddess,' I said, and she just gave me the sphinx smile that closes all arguments round here.

'Are you serious?' I say, as he pushes a pawn forward.

'You'd better be serious about my money,' says Nails, whose nickname refers to the time he nailed a business rival to a tree in Gramercy Park. Although we have only his word for this, Nails is six inches taller than my five foot eight, works out every day and has often hinted that he might want to maim us to save face in the local business community. Suddenly a trailer for *EastEnders* comes on the tube prompting me to fumble for the remote, which has performed its usual disappearing trick.

'You know what's happening in *EastEnders*, right?' says Nails, perking up suddenly.

'No!' I say firmly before he can get into that.

'But . . .'

'Absolutely not! I've no idea what's happening and I don't want to know.'

'Come on . . .'

'Look! You've heard of Fred West, right? English serial killer.'

A shrug.

'Killed twenty-five people. Maybe more.'

Nails doesn't even bother with a shrug this time, but inside my head I can hear the inevitable American comment: ' . . . but there's a guy in Texas who's killed seventy-five.'

'He raised a family in a cross between a whorehouse and a morgue,' I say. 'Even he wouldn't let his kids see *EastEnders*. Said it was too depressing.'

The shrug is back.

Suddenly a Lou Reed concert is on the television screen, which I never ever turn off, not even when I'm asleep. I concentrate hard on the man on the sound desk until I am sure he will get my astral e-mail. *Have another spliff, mate. Get your favourite comic book out and pretend you can read it. Do anything rather than actually listen to the band. Don't worry about the feedback: the audience doesn't know any better.* By the look of agony on Lou's face it's a fair bet that my attempts at sorcery have been rewarded, but I can't bear to turn the television up to find out. And Nails has some wisdom to share with me.

'You should never have let her buy all that coke,' he says, shaking his head.

'She makes her own decisions,' I say, with a surprising amount of edge. I didn't know I had any Sir Galahad in me but apparently so.

'Whatever,' says Nails. 'I never believed all that stuff from pussy-whipped college boys that women are the stronger sex. Who's the toughest motherfucker on the planet? Naomi Campbell? Madonna? Bullshit! Mike Tyson is the champ.'

'And he's gay,' I say, just to see what happens.

Nails gives me a sulphurous look. It's probably time to put a bulletproof vest on now that I have invoked the demon that black males fear most, but I feel lucky today.

'What about jail?' I say, heart fluttering a good deal faster. 'Didn't you have a wife in there?'

Time freezes. Eventually he says, 'I was calling the shots.'

His voice is slower and deeper now, but he would probably have preferred carving those words into my back.

'So it doesn't count if you're the active partner,' I say. 'And I thought I was in denial.' As I have turned the colour of rancid tofu I haven't really won this one. He sees the tremor in my hands and smiles.

The screeches from the baby monitor reach a new crescendo.

'That will be Prince Albert's magic wand,' I say. 'And today, just for a treat, Sasha's dipped it in peppermint oil.'

Nails knows what a Prince Albert is and it doesn't take long for him to work out where the wand is going to go, especially now that Rob is literally screaming for forgiveness.

'I blame the parents,' I say, as I move my white bishop. Now it has the potential sting of a peppermint-flavour kebab skewer inserted right where you need it least. Rob is in his own personal Armageddon right now, hollering fit to bust as they say down South. Nails shoots me a look and I turn the baby monitor down.

'Was that bothering you?' I say, but Nails doesn't dignify that with a reply. He knows I am trampling all over his thinking time and he wants to win today. But then so do I.

'It will be over soon,' I say and get the look in return, espresso strength. An Essex steroid dealer I used to know called it 'the eyeball screw'. Coming from a pumped-up black guy with a barely visible tattoo of the grim reaper on his right wrist it's quite frightening. So I shut up.

'Yes! No! No! No! Yes! Oooh!'

There is more, but the repetition is probably too much even for Steve Reich fans. Nails opens his mouth to speak and produces a gurgle of toxic phlegm. On the second attempt he says, 'It's time to use the videos of that guy. He's a rich man. And we are sitting here on our butts doing nothing about it.' But it's my move now and I have to concentrate. Nails obviously hasn't read the same book on openings as I did because one of his knights is proving especially aggravating. That gives me a good excuse to ignore this potentially disastrous scheme.

'He made the Forbes Five Hundred last year,' wheedles Nails, if a behemoth can be said to wheedle. The Bill Evans CD finishes and segues into a piece of ambient dance music I tricked my computer into composing – tinkling bells and samples of Sasha's softest sighs. It's very soothing, although it wouldn't matter much if it wasn't on at all. Whereas if one of the post-serialist pieces I have spent the last two decades composing was on, Nails would put a fist through my crooked English teeth, rip my lungs out and then deposit the still-twitching grey air sacs on the table in front of me. The reaction to my music used to give me a lot of grief. Actually I am lying here, something you're going to have to get used to: it still gives me a lot of grief. In a world where people think Bob Dylan is a musician and Mick Jagger is a singer, I suppose I shouldn't mind but it still rankles, even after all these years.

'Strange the way coffee has taken over from cocaine,' I say to Nails, as the machine is ready now. I realised before I had finished saying it that this was complete and utter nonsense, but you could imagine someone getting a magazine piece out of it.

'Where you been?' he says, eyeing his thimble-sized cup disdainfully. 'Try selling this stuff on the street and you're going to get nined.'

He takes a sip then nods his approval. 'You guys owe me money, right?'

'H'mm.'

'You have this product I can exploit, right? Rob's secret life as a john.'

'Yes! Yes! Yes! Yes!' says Rob, saving me the trouble.

'You want to sell T-shirts?' I say. 'Instructional videos?'

'The story must be worth something,' he says stubbornly. 'Didn't Rob go to England once? And meet the Royal Family?'

'He shook Prince Charles's hand at a charity benefit,' I say.

'So we get him to say he sucked Prince Andrew's dick or something.'

'Just why are the Windsor family so fascinating for you bloody colonials? What is the attraction? And who is interested in yet more celebrity depravity?' I say.

Nails's raised eyebrow points out the flaw in this.

'He hasn't had a hit for ages,' I say. 'Look, you can't blackmail him and sell him drugs at the same time.' Before I even finish the sentence I realise I am wrong again.

'You're just jealous of his bond with Sasha. What if she fell in love with him?' he says.

'This is payback for the gay stuff, right?' I say.

A one-sided smile alerts me to the fact that he has a lethal punch coming my way.

'What if he took her away from you?' he says. 'That would be a great angle for the press.' His hands block out an imaginary headline. 'Spider Black's widow escapes from evil pimp by marrying Rob Powers! I can just see the TV movie. It's perfect. No?' His smile widens as I slump in my seat. 'What goes around comes around,' says Nails, with a nod at Pazazu. 'You've been messing with some bad shit.'

I look for flaws in his gleaming white teeth but there aren't any.

'What would she do with millions of dollars?' I say. 'She's got me.'

Nails continues to radiate malevolence as I wriggle on the end of his hook.

'It's probably time to start doing the dishes and not just say I'm going to,' I say, but nothing will puncture that seraphic smile. Some time later I have lost the game of chess and most of my marbles, and I am sifting through every remark Sasha, Rob and Nails have ever made.

By the time Nails has left and Rob has limped off to lick his wounds Sasha has asked me if 'anything is wrong' many times but I can't possibly tell her.

She couldn't fall in love with Rob anyway. Could she? I watch her stride around the living-room watering the plants, singing as she does so. Why is she so happy?

'You couldn't fall for Rob,' I say eventually and watch very carefully. She laughs, a genuine unforced one. The sort you get when I put the wrong key in the lock, or rip open a bag of coffee so it goes everywhere, or slip on the soap in the shower stall, or . . . never mind, I know when she's not faking it.

'He's a client,' she says, shaking her head.

'What if he wasn't? I mean, he's a millionaire. Just about famous. Sort of handsome.'

'I have changed his diapers. How could I fall in love with him?'

'I'll buy that,' I say, and we embrace. Just as we are coming to the decision that there is something here worth exploring further, the terminally banal theme to *EastEnders* comes on the television. Sasha whoops with delight, which sends me out to check the answering machine. There's usually some fresh messages for Sasha but for once there's something waiting for me. Something so nasty I have to wind it back and listen to it again to see if it will get better with repetition.

It doesn't. The voice has been distorted by some electrical hocus-pocus, adding an extra chill to the content of the message.

'It has come to our attention that you have been exploiting the left-hand path for financial gain. The activities of parasites are usually of no interest, but you have used some of our material to falsely claim you are in some way affiliated to us. You will soon pay the price. Prepare to die.'

Which is all I need. Satanic fundamentalists.

I find the website address of the Satanists whose occult pitch I borrowed from and e-mail: 'Can't you take a joke?' They will probably be too busy sodomising headless chickens to answer anyway. In my innocence I thought that my Kathy Acker-style plagiarism was a 'homage'. But some people just don't seem to understand what post-modernism is all about. While I'm coping with that, not terribly well, Nails drops by to watch *EastEnders* with Sasha. I can't handle the two of them clucking away over life in Walford so I stay brooding in my den until it's over. 'I was going to play Nails the music for the new show,' says Sasha on my return.

'No!' I say, unwilling to cast pearls before swine.

'Play me some of your music, man,' says Nails, only because he knows I don't want to.

'You won't like it,' I say.

Sasha rolls her eyes. This is not the American way. 'It's brilliant, Nails,' she says, 'but you have to approach it in a different way.'

Nails trains his shades on me again. He knows he has a live one here.

'Put some on,' he teases.

'No,' I say, flatly and without aggression by my standards.

'OK. Simmer down, old boy.' This is said in what he believes to be a perfect British accent, in other words the voice of an effeminate homosexual upper-class pervert in about 1930.

'It would ruin our relationship,' I say.

'I'll pay you. Then you won't complain when I tell you what I really think.'

'I know already,' I say.

'Thirty dollars,' he says.

I pick up a tape of a piece that nearly crippled an English virtuoso pianist in rehearsal. He eventually resorted to altering the score hoping I wouldn't notice. This was written before computers enabled everyone to construct such things and is in four different time signatures simultaneously, not that anyone except me would ever know. To most people it sounds like one of those piano-smashing competitions they used to have.

'Cost you a hundred dollars, then you can say what you like,' I say.

He takes his shades off and looks at me for a long bowel-loosening moment.

'Your pupils are awfully big,' I say. 'It might be love. It might be drugs.'

'I'll give you a hundred bucks,' he says.

'It's drugs.'

'Let's take it off your tab,' he says. 'Say you owe me nine thousand and nine hundred dollars.'

It's a very generous offer. The only problem being I had no idea 'we' owed him that much. I look at Sasha pointedly.

'Who's been a busy little girl then?' I say, but there is not a flicker of guilt. I might as well be looking at a statue, a modern work entitled 'Fuck Off. And Die'. Somewhat irritated at Sasha's greedy little nostrils, I put the tape in the deck.

'Go on, take your best shot,' I say.

As the first deep rumblings of the piece sound out I feel some of that old familiar rage, knowing what the reaction is going to be. Nails consumes horror movies avidly, the sort that used to come complete with complex atonal orchestral soundtracks. So he is used to dissonance. But without a visual prop he will not be able to cope. And he doesn't.

One reaction to fear is hysterical laughter. Lots of it. Some of which I was expecting. But not this much. He is gasping for breath and literally holding his sides.

'I could run a copy off for you,' I say, after which it's some time before he can sit up again. It takes a long time for Nails to stop laughing, probably because my stone face sets him off again every time he looks in my direction.

'You went to college to study that?' he says.

'You know all this already,' I say, amazed at how much mileage Nails is getting out of this one.

But he won't let it drop. 'This is the "music that no one has ever heard before"? "No one can possibly guess what it's going to sound like"?'

I'm surprised he remembered my sales pitch, but I'm not flattered because he looks like he might literally crack a rib. He is gasping out loud and rolling around on the couch, one hand on his stomach. It's pissing Sasha off too, because she is on the side of Art in the war against the Philistines. As her work usually involves peeled-back labia it's easier for her to find a gig, but she too has felt the sting of public indifference.

'It's meant to be challenging, you dolt,' I say. 'It's an attempt to frustrate the expectations of the audience.'

'So it ain't no surprise then when there is no audience,' he says, on his third attempt.

'Not only no audience,' I say, 'but there is usually no perform-ance for them not to turn up to in the first place.'

'And you call that music?'

I think he is going to leak more than teardrops if he carries on like this.

'It's good to see I can reduce an audience to tears,' I say, as the senseless cackling continues.

'Shut up, you stupid nigger,' says Sasha suddenly. I'm shocked. She has never ever detonated that word in my presence. Nails just laughs louder. He carries on while Sasha storms out of the room before finishing off with some yuck yucking that would be tagged as politically incorrect if a white guy imitated it.

'She looks even prettier when she's angry. What does she see in you?' he says.

'Some call it love,' I say. 'It might happen to you one day.' Now he's back on his laughing hyena trip and it's really starting to grate. He knows this music is torn from the inside of my soul. He is well aware that I didn't just write it, I practically bled it on to the manuscript paper.

The front door slams.

There is a slight lull in the storm of hilarity then he forces himself to laugh again, which is really annoying.

'How long does this last?' he says, wiping his eyes.

If I told him the answer – two hours – it would probably kill him, and although nothing would please me more right now I have had enough. 'You going to fuck off now?' I say.

He shakes his head.

'Sasha said she would give me my money. I'm gonna wait.'

I look at him long enough to know that locking antlers would not be a good idea at this point.

As I storm out of the house I start to picture the death of Nails. I see him torn on a wheel, hung from a tree and torn apart by wild dogs. I see myself stabbing him repeatedly then carving his naked body into small bite-sized pieces. My blood sings inside me as I imagine the impact of warm, wet, spurting plasma on my face. 'If only,' I say out loud to a passing grey squirrel. And mean it.

I'm not the only guy cursing and muttering on this particular afternoon, but I'm probably the only one who hasn't yet been prescribed medication for his condition. To put the tin hat on it, it's Good Friday, which even in New York adds an extra pall of gloom to the proceedings. I remember that Rob is on a radio talk show, recorded live somewhere in Manhattan, and tune my walkman into it. Soon rage suffuses every cell of my body, but you know all that already.

After a long walk alongside the Hudson and a sojourn in a deli trying to read an English paper without bursting into nostalgic tears, I get back to the flat some three hours later. The air inside is not as fresh as it might be, and the closer I get to Sasha's Chamber the worse it is. Something worse than the usual old bodily fluids overlaid with disinfectant starts to push my panic button as I fumble for the lightswitch. There is a click but the bulb must have gone. I walk across the room in the dark and in the process trip over something soft and bulky on the floor. For those who believe that we create our reality by the exercise of will, what happens when I find the other lightswitch serves me right.

Nails is lying across the floor. But it's not Nails any more, it's just the husk, the shell; there's no one home any more. The starfire stuff, the spirit, the psyche, whatever you want to call it, has gone.

Sasha.

She wouldn't. She couldn't.

An image of her as Kali swims up from my memory bank, the poster for her new show which features her brandishing a bloodstained knife and baring her teeth. She has kohl-rimmed eyes, blue face make-up and in her left hand she is carrying what appears to be a bloodstained dildo. Several print firms turned the work down until she found a feminist group of art terrorists who chided her for going soft.

Why not use a lookalike dick? Or the real thing?

I wouldn't put it past the little imp to do something like this to drum up some more headlines, but this is not the time to be flippant. It's probably time to assume the foetal position and then fake insanity for the next couple of decades, but I feel strangely calm. It doesn't matter. I am standing in a pool of congealed blood but somehow still breathing deeply and slowly. Nothing will be achieved by running around like a headless chicken in any case.

'Well, I guess we have saved ten thousand dollars,' I say, but my voice sounds high and trembly. Then I remember it's nine thousand and nine hundred. Money won't leave you alone even in a room full of blood, a fluid that is now liberally spread around the room with my fingerprints.

I see guilt on my face as I look in one of the room's many mirrors. There is literally blood on my hands and I start to think about the fair trial we are going to get. Apart from my Satanic dabblings and Sasha's therapeutic practice, many think Sasha was lucky to get away with the last one. I know she didn't give Spider Black a fatal dose of heroin. She told me so. So what if her fingerprints were on the syringe? Maybe it was euthanasia. He certainly wanted to die. But that was then and this is now.

More information floods at me quicker than I can cope with it.

Nails is naked, face-down, hands cuffed behind his back. His clothes have been folded neatly next to the body. Averting my eyes just gets me the sight of Nails's penis, sawn off at the base and placed in the hand of a figurine of Seth, the supposedly evil deity Sasha likes to use as a prop sometimes. There is a brief interlude while I stand there clasping my own tackle and moaning aloud, but that won't get us out of this.

I remember the show she did which climaxed with the castration of Osiris. It was gory enough to get raided by the Michigan police and ensured renewal of her National Endowment for the Arts grant. I thought that was a brilliant piece of media manipulation. Now I'm not so sure.

Maybe this particular installation is what some call a homage. Or someone wants to get at Sasha, not to mention Nails, of course, but so many people must have wanted to kill him I wouldn't know where to start. I know for a fact he knocked his women about when they looked like leaving him or when he was high or when there was an 'r' in the month. Or a vowel for that matter.

And Sasha had wished him dead many a time. She was scared of him and didn't have the money to pay him, but even so . . .

Anyway, she was at the shops, as I was. A key in the lock announces Sasha's arrival.

'Sasha!' I shout.

'Hang on,' she says. 'I must make a phone call.'

Well, if she's faking innocence she's better at acting than I ever thought, and I've seen her stuff countless times plus what happens offstage, if any performer can ever be said to be offstage. I call her again.

'I'm coming, I'm coming,' she calls, meaning she isn't. Just yet. But will be in a minute. Maybe.

'Sasha!' My throat hurts after that one, but it gets her steel-tipped purple Docs clattering this way. I watch the doorway for her entrance knowing that her reaction to the carnage will be crucial.

That's when I notice that the ornamental chalice Sasha reserves for various sacred fluids is now full of blood. It's beginning to dawn on me that this is a human sacrifice, but before there is time to start gibbering Sasha strides in ready to rend my body asunder and eat the flesh.

'This had better be good . . .' she begins, then it hits her.

She gasps once and then her hands cover her face while she takes in every detail of the scene. It's surprisingly low key but then she's been here before. As I have, even though mine was just a lucky punch. The friends and family of the deceased might not have seen it that way, but as we left the country the next day we will never know. I never got to use my defence which was: 'He started it!'

I might have got away with manslaughter but I think the British police might have thought it was pushing the envelope just a tad to have danced on the face of the victim until it resembled a seafood pizza. So Sasha says anyway. I don't remember. I used to drink, you know.

In the process of defending Sasha's honour in a South London pub I killed the brother of a career criminal, the sort of guy with three current working aliases and membership of the same Masonic lodge as the top-ranking policemen who are supposed to be putting him behind bars. But that's the least of our problems right now. She is looking at me the way I am looking at her. There is only one question in the air, but neither of us wants to say it.

'Well, don't look at me,' I say. 'I just got back.'

She looks innocent, but then she went to drama school once upon a time. I put that out of my mind while Sasha launches into a history lesson.

'This looks like a fertility sacrifice,' she says, reminding me that Sasha is presently trying to conceive. This process now involves me sitting in baths of ice-cold water, although my sperms certainly used to work. If I were to say that maybe the problem is her womb she would probably kill me too.

I didn't say that or even think it.

Maybe something possessed her. Whether that would be a valid defence on a charge of murder in New York City remains to be seen.

'Sasha was just possessed by the ancient Egyptian spirit Seth, officer. You know. The one that eventually became the Xtian devil. Or maybe it was Pazazu. The scaly, winged terror we use as a hatstand. Remember *The Exorcist*?'

It is not looking good.

She looks down at the glistening blood and shivers. When she starts to cry it's like it will never stop. I still can't feel anything yet except that it's a good idea to hold her until she stops crying. While that's going on I stare intently at her collection of little teddy bears for which she made Egyptian costumes. There's Isis,

Osiris and cuddly little Seth with his ass's head. What would the prosecution make of that?

Not much later we have sniffles then an uneasy silence.

'Maybe you got one of your rituals wrong,' I say, trying to keep it light. She pushes me away and starts to say something that obviously has been bothering her a long time.

'Me? I told you this Satanic stuff would blow up in your face,' she says.

'Superstition brings bad luck,' I quote back, but she has won that one. It never felt right even if the money was good.

'Better ring the cops,' I say.

'We will solve this ourselves. We don't need them.'

'That's about as convincing as a government anti-drug campaign.'

'We can't have the police in here. This is my temple. This is where I do my work. I must purify the space.' She closes her eyes, 'centres' herself and starts to emit sounds that would have her committed to a padded cell most places in the known universe. Which gives me a chance to look at the body more closely.

His pockets are empty, least they are after I have trousered his roll of bills, and his Rolex has gone but I think we can rule out robbery on this one. Occult hygiene would recommend burning the bills, but I feel the fiscal energy would be better off in circulation.

'Alas, poor Nails,' I say, then wonder why I am talking to myself. It's probably to block out the keening, wailing sounds Sasha is making. Astral house-cleaning is hard on the ears, so to take my mind off the weeping and wailing I kneel down next to the body to try to read what has been carved into the back. These are cabbalistic symbols, familiar hocus-pocus to me or to anyone else who has ever visited an occult bookshop. They mean so many different things to followers of different traditions that it's pointless trying to decipher them, but I make a note of them. They look familiar because Sasha has used all this stuff in her show, which sets the alarm bells ringing again but she could not have done this. I think of the way deluded mothers of mass murderers always refuse to believe that their boy could have done such a thing, then I force myself to start on the body.

Convulsed by the dry heaves, I somehow pick the prick up, that is to say the detached organ and not Nails himself.

'Put that in the freezer,' says Sasha, index finger jabbing the air as it always does when she is giving orders.

'In case you feel peckish later?' I say, gagging somewhat.

'We need the whole body,' she says. 'Remember the Osiris myth?'

'Who needs to remember it? We're living it.'

Her eyes flash dangerously and as her mouth opens I realise we could spend the next three weeks exploring Ancient Myths and their Contemporary Relevance. I get in first.

'Maybe we should send it to his main squeeze,' I say.

'She probably cut it off,' says Sasha.

'Who was she?' I say, all excited now it seems we have a clue. Who better than the battered lover to perform this grisly deed?

Sasha just shrugs.

'He never seemed to fall in love except with himself.'

'That's right. The women were just a business thing.'

'He was a pain in the ass while he was alive and he's a bigger pain now that he's dead,' I say.

'Maybe that should go on his tombstone.'

Which reminds me we still have a cadaver on our hands. And I am still holding a second-hand organ of reproduction.

'He called it his Johnson. Remember?' she says.

'No, I don't,' I say, somewhat frostily. I wonder how many

cosy little chats they had about his Johnson. I put it in the freezer then wash my hands, but I have to scrub to get the blood out of my fingernails. I tell myself not to look in the mirror but then I do anyway, and I see that presence that has always seemed to be lurking inside me. It's the part of me that thought it was a great idea to stomp on that guy's head until his life leaked out. I straighten up and tell myself to behave then go and stare at what used to be Nails again.

If I turn it over I am going to be confronted with a blackened serrated void where Nails's pride and joy used to hang. And no doubt much more. But some insistent voice inside me wants to see what our nemesis has wrought, so I quickly flip the body and then puke all over it. Sasha opens her eyes to tell me off for being a wuss then sees the crusted black blood where his penis used to be. Among the banshee voices in my head are the distorted tones of the phone message. 'You will soon pay the price. Prepare to die.'

'Let's ring the police,' I say. 'Let them do what they're good at.'

I didn't mean it and I'm glad when Sasha rolls her eyes round her head.

'This never happened,' she says. 'It's Nails's problem. Nothing to do with us. We get rid of the body. That's it.'

I want this to be true but some scepticism must be showing on my face because a sudden burst of rage infuses her next statement.

'Once they start digging they are going to find out a lot of stuff about us.'

Like the fact that you did this murder, some voice whispers inside me.

'The first thing we have to do is to check your household slaves,' I say, and to my intense surprise Sasha actually agrees with me for once. While I'm still reeling from the shock of her acquiescence Sasha starts to giggle then puts a hand over her mouth.

'Go on. Tell us. I could do with a laugh,' I say.

'It's just the thought that Christian or Gabriel could do this. They're both such wimps.'

'Beat it out of them,' I say.

'Then they'll never talk,' she says, trotting out that old chestnut, although there are plenty of masochists who don't like pain at all. Indeed, some of them have got so many rules and regulations it's hardly worth bothering. I might be a slave but you're not going to boss me about is their attitude. I ask you.

'It may seem obvious,' says Sasha, 'but what if Nails just opened the door and let someone in? It just needed someone with a good pitch on the doorstep.'

'Yeah. Like, "Pizza! Extra olives and heavy on the garlic!" Why not open the door? Why would a six foot two tough guy be afraid of anything?'

'Let's just pack our bags and leave the country.'

'We already did that once. This is your greatest opportunity, right? Tell your occult groupies they can play with a dead body. Drink his blood. Wow! That's really fashionable right now!'

She does seem to be taking this rather too well.

'Are you sure you didn't do this?' I say, which has her waving her hands about in an especially demented way.

'Excuse me? Like *you* couldn't have done it,' says Sasha. 'You were ready to kill. I've seen that look in your eyes before.'

Which shuts me up.

'Somebody must have seen someone entering the flat,' I say after a quick sulk.

'What about your Satanic stalker? The adept can always achieve invisibility when required,' says Sasha, more or less seriously.

'In that case I must be the greatest magus on earth,' I say, bitter gall spreading through my body and soul. 'All anyone has to do is write some music no one has ever heard before and the cloak of invisibility will automatically descend.'

'You always say that,' she says, which is true. I always say that. We leave the wreckage of my career behind and get on with it.

'We have to do something,' I say, helpful as ever.

'Call the police?' she says, words dripping with irony.

'I fell over the corpse so there's my prints, hairs, and whatever connecting me to it. We owed him money and in the eyes of the law we are both criminals. Your prints are probably on those cuffs. We should wait.'

'Yeah, right. It's Good Friday. Maybe he will rise on Easter Sunday.'

Our eyes lock and I realise that we are now bonded tighter than we have ever been. We are still in love and we certainly can't complain of the tedium of married life right now. Every cloud has a silver lining.

'Maybe it's Rob Powers, Prince of Darkness. All this time I never realised he was a Satanic Adept,' I say witheringly.

Sasha's withers remain unwrung.

'He's a lot smarter than Nails,' she says. 'Maybe he got him to take his clothes off then surprised him.'

'He was doing live radio while it was happening. I even listened to it on my walkman. What are we going to do?' I say, starting to whine a little and do a bit of hand-waving myself.

'We get rid of the body and no one will ever miss Nails. Let's start with the dick,' she says, practical as ever.

'Let's fry it. It should taste better than those vegetarian sausages you keep buying.'

The thought occurs to me that maybe she already knows what

the organ in question tastes like but now is not the time to voice my suspicions.

'Remember when we shared that we had both killed someone?' I say. Lightning flashes briefly. 'By accident,' I add soothingly.

She nods.

'It sort of bound us together in a strange way. It's like there's always a bit like that at the start of a relationship where you swap old wounds. Maybe it's to see if the other person is going to heal them or not.'

'Unless you are looking to be wounded further,' says Sasha.

'That's right. Not everyone is looking for a happy ending.'

'Otherwise I would be out of a job,' she agrees.

'I suppose he'll haunt us now,' I say, still jabbering to try to keep my mind off things. Neither of us believes in hauntings or what most punters understand by the occult or black magic.

Sasha shakes her head. 'This is just a garbage-disposal problem. But let's make some money off him first.'

This is my moment to share that I am five thousand dollars richer, but I just can't do it.

'Remember he always said he wouldn't be seen dead in here,' she says.

We manage a pair of weak smiles then settle back to puzzling a way out of this.

'Let's start with Christian and Gabriel,' I say.

'They would never disobey me,' she says, but while she is saying it some of the steam goes out of it until she finishes with that typically American rising cadence to signify a question.

'Ring them,' I say, pronouncing it the same way, which prompts her to give me the finger.

While she's gone to terrorise her slaves I realise that Nails will fit in our brand-new freezer. If we fold him before he goes stiff and eat a lot of spinach dhansak in the near future. I start to clear a space for Nails's shell by stacking up frozen vegetarian meals next to the freezer.

'I just remembered they went to Christian's parents for Easter.' What are you doing?' says Sasha, on her return.

'Got a better idea? He's going to start to smell in a day or so.'

'Remember *Weekend at Bernie's*? You used to love that movie,' she says as I grab hold of the feet.

'I used to drink,' I say. I can't imagine giggling at a regular moron fest like that these days. In fact I may never smile again the way things look right now. I manage to fold Nails neatly in the freezer and then not throw up as stuff leaks from the corpse.

'Gross,' says Sasha helpfully, but at least she helps me sponge the blood up. Soon only a forensic scientist or the person who did this would ever know there had been a grisly murder committed in this space. But it still doesn't feel right.

'What do we do now? Light a stick of incense or something?' I say.

Her face lights up in a way I have grown to dread.

'There's one way we could cleanse this space,' she says, with the little minx smile that usually signals something dangerous or illegal is about to happen. A much-derided love poem written by a previous swain who died in her arms comes to mind.

' "Your dimples wax and wane like miniature moons",' I quote, and her smile widens.

'What about these miniature moons?' she says and swivels around to face away from me. She is wearing skin-tight pink rubber pants which are perfect for turning the axis of her pelvis from side to side and round and round. Slowly, then quicker, she varies the parameters often enough to hypnotise this particular onlooker, even though I've seen it before.

When she turns her head her lipstick is glistening. 'What are you waiting for?' she breathes.

As I move forward my shoes stick to the floor, which is still slightly tacky with Nails's blood. Loud alarm bells are ringing inside my head: this isn't exactly appropriate behaviour.

'It's only because your parents are Bible-bashers you take such delight in trying to shock,' I say, trying to defuse the situation before she suggests having a threesome with a dead dickless drug dealer.

'State the fucking obvious, why don't you?' she says happily. Each shift of her slight body reminds me I am powerless when she does this stuff. 'It's three o'clock too,' she informs me.

It's a while before I realise that this is still Good Friday and three o'clock is a defining moment for a lot of people. Her skewed smile is stronger now and has won me over completely.

This is undeniably childish; it's just transgressing against the laws of a dead religion – so what? It's still fun none the less. 'The devil made me do it,' I say.

'Get thee behind me. And rub my buns. Ooh! That's nasty,' she says, in a half-croak when I have done so. 'Come on. Do I have to draw you a diagram?'

I give in and do what she wants. A familiar scenario.

It occurs to me while enacting the Great Rite that if the police were to arrive now it wouldn't look very good for us, but I manage to concentrate somehow. If you believe that children are influenced by the state of mind of the parents during their conception, then we could also be spawning a monster here. Sasha has drifted off somewhere, in a trance so deep I fear she might never return. She always was a show-off at this point, but this time her fevered growls and screeches are of a frightening intensity. It may mean orgasmic bliss, it may mean she wants to scream and shout a lot. It's hard to tell. In general, she's hard to figure out.

As she pounds the floor with her fists and explores the

extremes of her five-octave vocal range your old-time wise persons might expect the name of the killer to appear magically at this point. Apparently the astral jury is still out on that one, for the storm eventually subsides without any startling revelations.

I conserve my yang just as recommended in Sasha's Tantric manuals, and after she has given freely of her yin we pause to catch our breath.

When it's finally safe to uncouple we repair to the other room to take stock of the situation. It's time to earth ourselves with a nice cup of Assam tea with organic honey.

As if we were both British we pretend we haven't just made love exactly where a dead body lay. It's for the best.

'If we did call the police . . .' I say.

'Look at it this way,' she says, holding a hand aloft to signify that this is an important statement and I had better shut the fuck up. 'This is a great opportunity for us. You know those creepy rich clients of yours who want to "cross the abyss". What would they pay to play with a dead body? This is such an amazing business opportunity I can hardly believe it.'

'Do they have the chair or lethal injection in New York?' I ask, but she waves that one away with one of her red-taloned hands. 'Well in your case they will probably burn you alive,' I say.

'Electrocution often is burning alive. It can take five minutes to roast you to death,' she says.

Our eyes lock while we consider the magnitude of this particular gamble. It really is a matter of life and death.

'You can always say you were abused . . .'

'I *was* abused,' she reminds me icily.

'Yes, yes, but what is my excuse going to be?'

'The devil made you do it,' she says, cutely modelling a pair of horns on her head with raised index fingers. She holds the pose for a long time with an especially winning smile.

'That really suits you,' I say.

'That's right,' she says. 'The devil is a woman.' She says that reverently enough for me to realise it's from her patron saint, the blessed Camille Paglia. Just then I notice that she has yet to empty the chalice of blood. In fact she has written something in it with her fingers right where Nails died.

DIE YOU PIG it says next to an inverted pentagram. I stand rooted to the spot, unsure of whether I even want to carry on breathing.

'It's a joke,' she says. 'I thought you would think it's funny. It's a joke. I didn't kill him. This is just a joke.'

Time passes while she keeps on repeating herself, tugging at my arm like a spoiled brat.

'If you say so, dear,' I say, and wander off to get a fresh sponge.

2
Good Friday Night

'I MUST HAVE A soak in the tub,' says Sasha. 'Can you clean up?'

As she knows this is the last thing I want to do, all the black arts of a 1950s starlet come into play: the wiggle, the pout, even a giggle or two. Then as soon as she sees I am about to do her bidding she shifts up a gear. 'Don't lose any blood,' she says, voice hardening into her lucrative Bitch Queen of Belsen persona. 'Use a sponge. Don't miss a single drop.'

Sasha has always been good at delegation but sometimes the tone of her voice leaves just a little bit to be desired. I thought my last five-day sulk had established that there is a difference between me and those who come to pay homage to her supreme majesty, but we seem to have run into a spot of cognitive dissonance. I cup my hands round my mouth, fill my lungs and interface with her nearest ear.

'Hello! Sasha! It's me! Remember?'

She wrinkles her nose, winks as if to say, What's all the fuss about? A particularly winning smile relaxes me momentarily and then she's back snapping at my ankles again. 'Go on, then,' she says, mystified as to why I'm still there. I can't let it pass.

'Why don't you leave the blood where it is and call it a work of conceptual art?' I say, knowing she does not like undue levity on the subject of Her Work. The irony, if that was what it was, doesn't even touch her. She stares past me as she shares the idea with whatever deity is pulling her strings today.

' "Ritual Murder by Sasha Kristinson. Etching on Flesh Canvas. Limited Edition",' I say, although I am looking at a raised middle digit half-way through.

'Yeah. The NYPD would have something to say about that,' she says, with more than a twinge of regret in her voice. 'At least if you got fried I would get the covers of *Time* and *Newsweek*.'

'It's nice we can still share a joke. Of course, in another ten years or so – the time it would take to get me to the chair – or the needle or whatever, you won't need to resort to sensationalism to kick-start your career. You will already be famous.'

For the first time she looks offended. I should know there are some things you just don't joke about.

'I could throw you to the wolves,' she says. 'I just have to say you did it. Tell them you did that guy in Lewisham.'

As far as I can tell, that is to say not very far at all, her mind just skated over the possibility of betraying me purely for humorous purposes or as payback for the ultimate blasphemy of suggesting that she might not ever be successful. It's not like she would actually do it. Not at all. Better change the subject.

'Remember telling me about how the touch of a murderer's hand would cure the plague? What would a touch of Nails's Johnson cure?' I say.

'Do you really want me to tell you?' she says, with the widest smile I have seen all day.

'You never succumbed to his charms,' I say.

'Just keep telling yourself that.' A shadow of fear steals across her face, and I unclench my fists and try and lose the Aleister Crowley stare that sometimes claims me when I'm on the losing side of one of these amusing little exchanges.

'How could you think that?' she says, again with far too much sympathy in her face and voice. The inference is clear. I am losing my mind.

'Maybe I should just plead insanity,' I say.

'Then you would be the Psycho Pimp Killer,' she says breathlessly. We really must stop reading the Murdoch tabloids.

'Even worse, I would be the English Psycho Pimp Killer. Who enslaved an American beauty.'

Sasha takes a critical look in the mirror, probably seeing a bloated, wrinkled crone, especially now as she is facing thirty. She was not cheered by the quiet dignity with which I faced my second thirty-ninth birthday. She is terrified of the passage of time. Her magazine profiles tend to say things like: spiky blonde hair, luminous green eyes, cheekbones you could shave with, wide mouth, boyish frame, big lips and a slight but adorable gap between her front teeth.

They don't mention the things that twang my heartstrings like: laughing too loud, having a slightly prominent nose that contravenes the American limits for female pulchritude just enough to be really interesting, and the way her accent keeps floating across the Atlantic and back, usually depending on how much she likes me at any given time.

'You're not serious about using Nails to enslave our little flock,' I tell Sasha, who is running a bath scented with jasmine, neroli and some Mickey Mouse bubble bath. The bathroom is lit only by candles, some of them sailing about in little shells on the surface of the fragrant water. She tilts her head to one side and lets me look for my reflection in her eyes. I still can't decide if they are turquoise, grey-emerald or some shade of jade, but it's fun finding out.

'This will be so good,' she says dreamily. 'Pity we can't invite the critics. But just wait for the word-of-mouth business after tomorrow night.'

Which is what I'm worried about. 'I sort of preferred the traditional method of dealing with murder, which is keeping it a secret.'

'You're full of shit,' she says, then closes her eyes and dips her head under the water, letting her upturned palms break the surface of the water, to remind me of some old picture in the Tate Gallery. Vaguely remembering some story that the model died because the painter kept her in a cold bath too long, I can't help thinking that it would be the work of a moment to hold her head under the water long enough for ... No. I can't think what gets into me sometimes.

'There used to be a thriving market in relics from dead criminals, the hand of a hanged man, that sort of thing,' I say. 'We have got Nails's dick. Maybe if we spin it round ...'

'Like a ouija board?' she says dismissively. 'I told you I'm not superstitious.'

'No. "This is occult science",' I say, quoting from her own dissertation on retroactive sorcery, a little-known backwater of contemporary physics.

'You know we said we would finish that video for John Haskins,' I say, expecting a rueful smile and some statement along the lines of, 'Well at least we won't have to do that now. What a relief!'

She suddenly sits up in the bath, displacing water over the side and dousing a few of the floating candles. 'Oh my God. I promised John.'

'So what?'

'We are professionals. We must deliver. He said he might help us with the movie. And we have the interview with Rob tomorrow. On cable.'

I was forgetting that Sasha isn't likely to let a little thing like ritual murder get in the way of appearing on public-access television.

'Is that still a go project?' I say, tentatively as she doesn't like negativity, most especially when her career is concerned.

'Of course!' she says, pulling the plug briskly and calling for hot towels, coffee and make-up.

This is going to be a foot fetishist vid; nothing can happen really except Sasha taking her shoes on and off. The star, temperamental despite her minimal responsibilities, takes for ever to paint her toenails, after which she only needs to select a pair of shoes. About an hour later I'm contemplating making a few incisions myself with Sasha's ritual knife. Eventually she is crossing and recrossing her legs, and dangling her high heels off the tips of her toes while I stand around wondering why I'm massaging her ego when I'm doing all the work.

'Are you sure these are the right shoes?' she says.

'Yes!' I say, a little bit on the terse side.

The shoes are shiny and red, the heels high enough to induce permanent injury, and were probably designed by an unemployed chiropodist hoping to snag a few extra punters.

'Just *love* the heart-shaped padlocks,' I say, but she's in a downward spin. I wasn't quick enough with the reassurance, and now we are going to have a genuine attack of artistic temperament.

'You know I've stopped taking sweeteners in my espresso,' says Sasha, as she kicks whatever is closest across the room. 'I've told you a million fucking times!' Blood-red talons wave about very close to my bloodshot eyeballs. I can smell her coffee-charged breath.

'I'm not your fucking servant!' I say. 'Make your own coffee!'

The lengthy and fervent reply to that involves personal abuse there is no need to go into here. All the time it's happening I'm wondering whether this is the rage that killed Nails. Eventually I say: ' . . . And when your movie gets made.'

She lapses into shamefaced silence.

There actually was an attempt to make her life into an independent movie. We could have had cameo roles from the likes of Rob and many other Lower East Side luminaries and there was real money on the table. Sasha could make you believe that Michelle Pfeiffer would star in the remake in a few years' time, and for a while she wasn't really talking to me because I was not a movie star and she was. Then as the finance mysteriously disappeared, probably up someone's nose, she was going to do it herself and get Rob to fund it, which was not entirely unreasonable as he already published her book of poetry. It's called *Rusted Uterus* and we still have a few copies left if you're interested.

'Why did I say I would do this?' she says, trying to kiss and make up again.

'Because you are vain? And greedy?'

'Like you're not both those things.'

She eventually consents to sit still on a stool where I have lit the shot.

'Right,' I say. 'This isn't one of your hobbies. This is work.'

She writhes in agony straight away.

'Like you don't have crazes,' she says.

'Mine last longer than ten seconds. What happened to your tap-dancing? Then that dumb fucking personal astrologer. Then trepanation.'

'I'm still going to have that done.'

'Yeah, well, you need that like you need a hole in the head.'

'You've already said that. How long is this crap going to take anyway?' Somehow managing to imply that she could be shooting a much better movie somewhere else.

'Maybe two hours,' I say. 'And don't start asking me what your motivation is. You take the shoes off. You put them back on again. That's it. Make sure your stocking seams are straight.'

That is just about the only rule, although for all I know there is a subdivision of the market catering for people who like crooked seams and bunions.

I make sure the screen will be filled with a close-up of her gently wiggling toes rather than take one of her death-ray stares. The price of this video will be roughly three times what people will pay to see fit, attractive young people perform improbable and acrobatic sexual stunts in a bewildering variety of combinations, but that's niche markets for you.

'I think I've got enough footage now,' I say eventually, which prompts an exasperated groan from Sasha. One of her shoes comes winging swiftly past my head.

'That's not as cute as you think it is,' I say, but unfortunately it is. I'm still under her spell.

'I'm your *sole* reason for existing?' she says, which hurts more than the shoe would have.

'We really should talk about getting rid of the body,' I say. 'Let's get Jason Skinner. Fly him over. He's a useful man in a crisis.' Sasha looks blank until she remembers that Jason is the brother of the guy I killed in a drunken haze.

'He's your bogeyman, right?' says Sasha. 'The one you're so scared of.'

'He's killed a lot of people. Actually on purpose. Unlike us.' Though you probably meant to kill Nails when you drained all the blood out of him by cutting off his dick. I'll pretend that didn't occur to me.

'I heard he's a Rob Powers fan,' she says.

'How would you hear that?'

'While you were still drunk all the time before we fled the country. I made some enquiries among my girlfriends.' I visualise the ragbag of drug-addled, drunken whores Sasha is referring to and humbly beseech Odin that we should never set eyes on any of them again. 'He goes to a lot of prostitutes, usually two at a time,' says Sasha. 'When he's not talking about his muscles or doing drugs he's obsessing about Rob Powers. He knows everything about him.'

'Not as much as you do,' I say.

'Yeah. I could get Rob to move the body,' she says.

'Rob would do it then tell the police. You get off because you were abused as a child. I get fried, you marry Rob and live happily ever after. Until you arrange for another convenient drug overdose.'

Her eyes flash, which tends to confirm my suspicions that the death of Spider Black may not have been an accident. Still, if I had been there it would have been nothing like as quick and painless as a heroin overdose. I would have nailed him to the floor then used a jackhammer on his nuts and . . . where was I?

'It would be great to pin it on someone else,' says Sasha.

'This is getting like a chain letter. Someone dumps on us, we pass it on.'

'Shush now. We need a sacrificial lamb.'

'But Jesus has already died for our sins,' I say. She is not amused.

'A willing dupe,' she says, clicking her fingers to facilitate thought. 'Someone to take the rap.'

'You mean we plant the body in their house or something? Isn't that just a little bit risky?'

'So is sitting down in the electric chair. Some guys never get up again.'

'I'm so glad you mentioned the chair again. I just spent all of three minutes not thinking about it.'

Her index finger is pointing right at me yet again. 'Well, then. Prioritise. What about JC?'

I close my eyes and groan at the invocation of the Beast, in this case a poorly house-trained roadie with a bad case of the hots for Sasha. He would indeed do anything she said whatever the risk. She's right: he's a perfect choice.

'Not him,' I say, thinking of the deep psychic wounds I sustained during a week on the road tour managing for Rob. JC is a roadie from central casting, starting with the steel briefcase festooned with tour stickers, the jailer's keyring hanging from the belt of his putrid-smelling Levi's and the hundreds of Holiday Inn room keys he kept in his lair, which is still with his mom on Long Island. He's always trying to join our gang, but Sasha won't let him. She can't stand the smell. For reasons best known to himself JC thinks he is a Hell's Angel. Known only as JC, I was surprised to see that according to his passport his given name is John Hamilton Charles Jefferson III, a legacy of his hyper-rich father who seems to have faded from the picture as soon as he realised what he had sired.

'No, no,' I say, as his vision comes ever closer to materialising before my eyes.

'We could always pray for help,' says Sasha.

Without another word I find his phone number and he's so keen he is going to drive over right away.

I check through the spyhole that it is indeed JC and not our

Satanic nemesis or the NYPD. Apart from the addition of more facial flab, he has not changed: cut-down Levi jacket, inverted pentagram pendant, piggy eyes, long greasy hair with the hint of a monk's tonsure developing, wispy beard.

'I saw you made the latest GQ cover,' I say.

'That OK, chromedome. You need me,' he says. 'I don't know what it is. But you need me. And if I don't get any respect I'm out of here. I ain't kissing any butt.'

I wait while the sulphur fumes die out before replying. He hates me so much the plants in the hallway are practically wilting, but just as I can't push him any further I can't back down either.

'There's one butt you wouldn't mind kissing, right?' I say. 'She'll see you now.'

I offer him my back as I lead him through the hallway up to Sasha's lair. He manages to accompany me without plunging a knife between my shoulder blades but it's probably touch and go. I feel the 'What does she see in him?' vibe as I so often do from the motley collection of freaks who come to call for Sasha's therapy and, as always, it cheers me up.

Sasha has chosen to manifest with her hair pinned back and wearing a dark green robe into which is woven the occasional red rose. It's probably some reference to the goddess Venus, whose day it is today, and the red is for the wise blood. Or maybe it is for the blood of our sacrificial lamb now safe in our freezer ready for when our friends come to play. The chief manifestation JC is interested in is Sasha's cleavage – milk-white, fragrant, pushed up and out to invite but eternally out of reach to the malodorous buffoons with heavy keys dangling from their waists.

JC strides over towards her until her force field is enough to repel him. He halts half-way over the room. If he had a hat he

would be doffing it respectfully now; as it is he contents himself
with folding his hands over his big belly.

'That smell is you?' says Sasha, direct as ever. 'Are you serious?
You doing it for a bet? Two words for you. Soap and water.'

JC juts his big gut out further and puts his hands on his hips.

Half of him would like to teach her a lesson. Probably something non-consensual, painful and humiliating. The other half
of him wants to be stripped, whipped, hog-tied, cuffed and left
on her floor until she has drained every drop of sperm he will
ever produce. All of that is flickering away on his stubbly, blotchy
face while he replies. 'Soap and water is three words,' he says.

'Like Vidal Sassoon's Wash and Go. And the one he is marketing for roadies. Go and Wash,' says Sasha, aptly customising
an oldie but a goodie.

'What is this? Tea and crumpets with Mummy and Daddy?
I thought you guys were Satanists,' he spits and for once that
isn't an exaggeration.

'You're spitting at me, motherfucker. The price just went up.
And if you don't smell nice tomorrow you don't get in. Got it?'

He holds her gaze but his shoulders droop slightly.

Veneration of the feminine is where some types of witchcraft
cross over with s/m, so he is going to have to get used to it if
he ever wants to fulfil his grubby little fantasies of naked bodies
dancing around an open fire.

'If you wish to serve Satan, our Lord and Master, you will
first have to serve us. We wish you to dispose of one who has
displeased us.'

That gets his attention, all right. He steals a look at me to
check if this is for real, and I manage to keep a straight face.
Then he turns back to the source of real power in this room,
presently daintily stirring her nettle tea.

'If you are afraid, leave now; the path will be progressively more difficult from here on in,' she says. 'If you persevere, you will be rewarded beyond your wildest dreams. Once you cross the abyss there is no turning back.'

She's good at this. I feel the chill in the air as JC practically rolls on his back with his paws in the air waiting to have his tummy tickled.

'I am ready to serve,' he says, his voice deeper and noble. I suppose he is somewhere in a sword and sorcery comic now or in one of the well-thumbed slave planet sci-fi books he reads constantly.

'Very well,' says Sasha and produces an ornamental dagger with a few cabbalistic squiggles daubed on it in red fluid. It is not the weapon that is stored atop her altar in the Chamber, presumably because He Is Not Worthy. She opens up a scar on her right shoulder, drains a few drops into a gold chalice, then passes the knife to me. As I cut into one of the many scars on my arm I stare directly at JC. I know he isn't going to have a problem with the cutting of his flesh, but will he want to drink our blood? It's a harmless fluid compared with what's in the hamburgers and hot dogs he wolfs down every day, but you would be surprised how squeamish people are about such things. I pass him the knife and the cup. He hesitates once more but cuts into the top of his wrist and watches while his blood mingles with ours in the chalice. However rational you claim to be it's still a moving moment.

'Drink,' she says. There's not much in the cup but he drains it and hands it back to Sasha, who coyly turns her back on us, squats down and fills it. Now I see the need for the robe. She can fulfil this task without JC getting a look at the sacred mystery. She stands and hands him the bowl, eyes twinkling.

'It's got blood in it,' he says.

'Who's a lucky boy, then?' she says. 'Blood is the secret of women's mystic power, the sign of our union with the goddess, and in any case it's probably got more minerals and vitamins than the last thing you drank, which was . . .?'

'A can of Bud,' he says.

'Well, then.' She turns to me. 'Satanic liturgy just hasn't been the same since the AIDS crisis.'

He is still hesitating.

'If you're a scaredy cat you can't get in,' says Sasha.

JC quickly kneels at her feet and takes it, closes his eyes and breathes deeply of the clear nectar then quickly swills it down. Sasha just sits there in full Cleopatra mode with her glittering eyes saying something to me I don't want to hear right now, something like 'I got more disciples than you'. When he has drained the last drop he looks up at her.

'You don't have to lick the chalice, slave,' she says. 'You are now a novice. You will take orders from the adepts.'

He's not too happy with that but manages a nod.

'You must also carry our brand,' I say gravely.

I just made this up, but I know Sasha is going to go with it. Who wouldn't want to see a porker like JC gritting his teeth while his flesh sizzles? I hold out my arm to show him my latest brand at which, and for the first time ever, some measure of respect shows on his face.

'Only when we have seared your flesh will you be ready,' I intone, trying not to look at myself in the mirror in case I crack up. You can tell he can hardly wait to get started, but Sasha will no doubt fill his head with ritual codswallop while I'm off heating up the branding iron on the kitchen stove. Close at hand are cotton-wool pads, aloe gel and bandages, but I decide we won't bother with all that. JC can take his branding like a man.

I prop the lightning flash brand in the gas flame then realise I don't want him to have the same brand as me. Which leaves us

with a problem. Whatever I brand him with I will be responsible
for the consequences for all time. Something demeaning and he
will seek revenge. Equally, I don't want to elevate him above his
appropriate slave status. Which is all a distraction from the real
issue of making it hurt as much as possible. While the largest
trident shape we have is heating up, it's hard not to think of the
fun opportunities that might come our way now JC is on board.
We practise consensual sado-magic in our little coven, but it
would be a lie to suggest that other, darker fantasies never swim
up from Sasha's unconscious. If there should be an opportunity
to watch JC suffer for his many sins against humanity, and
against me in particular, I will be taking a front-row seat and a
souvenir T-shirt.

When the brand is ready I pull on my gloves and ring the
deeply sonorous handbell that will alert Sasha to the fact that it
is showtime. Shortly after, Sasha leads JC into our humble little
kitchen.

'This is the last thing. Then you get to play with the body,'
says Sasha.

'Play with it?' he says.

'Like you don't want to? Come on! Your secret is safe with
us.'

'He's a dead nigger. Why would I want to touch him?'

He knows he's not supposed to use that word as Sasha hit
him the last time but he's game, I'll give him that. There is a
red-hot iron waiting for wherever we decide to put it, and he is
still trying to piss us off.

'Oh my, you are a naughty boy,' says Sasha. 'Mummy is
shocked. But if I order you to suck Nails's dick you will do it.'

By the look on his face JC looks close to making excuses then
banging on the door of the nearest church that will have him.

'You must learn to confront what you fear most,' I say, staring at him, trying to conjure up the spectre of dread homosexual initiation rites, but he's too busy mutely worshipping Sasha to notice. Besides, even if all our gang have 'crossed the abyss' in a sexual sense, we might decide to waive this requirement for JC, who not only sports a ginger beard but usually also has crumbs in it.

'Are you ready?' I say, eager for him to feel the burn.

He steps up to the stove and offers me his arm. Our eyes lock for a long moment. Bestowing or receiving the kiss of fire should be a mystical experience, but something about the sight of JC reduces it to the level of flipping hamburgers.

'My executioner's hood is still at the dry-cleaner's,' I say.

'That's OK,' says JC. 'It's more frightening looking at your face.'

Sasha and I exchange a look.

'Never piss off a guy with a hot branding iron,' I say, but he is not going to back down. His eyes close as his flesh sizzles, but he makes no sound other than a strangled yelp. I wonder whether I have saved myself a special full body branding in the chair by admitting JC to our gang. The odour of seared flesh reminds me of the further possibility that I might just have doomed JC to the slow sizzle alongside myself.

'Welcome, brother,' I say.

3
Easter Saturday Morning

THE GUY UPSTAIRS has been up all night too, feeding his horror film habit. His heavy boots trace a path to the fridge or to the can whenever necessary, but apart from that he seems to do nothing besides grunt and groan theatrically while doom-laden music overlaid with screams and pistol-shots define the parameters of his never-changing world. I've sometimes seen his frizzy hair and shaggy overcoat at the video store; otherwise he seems to shun the society of human beings and I can't say that I blame him. Look where it gets you.

Church bells ring and horses whinny overhead, and I can almost see that path through the forest at Bray studios which features somewhere in just about every Hammer flick. As dawn breaks I give up thinking I am going to go to sleep and switch from decaff to the real thing.

What with our new house guest I can't seem to settle. I don't mean the corpse in the freezer, I mean the newly discarnate entity who has come to stay. Although most occultists will tell you that spirits don't hang around near their old containers, Nails is definitely inside my head and also hovering everywhere in the flat. I see him behind me in the mirror when I shave, he stands by the bed as I try to sleep, and a miniature version of him is lurking in the Roach Motel with the other cadavers. I take my coffee and sit down opposite Pazazu to see what he is thinking.

'Hi, buddy,' I say. 'You look a bit stressed today. You know who did this? Wanna share?'

Like he gives a shit, says Sasha from inside my head. This is disconcerting, the way her voice has been coming through loud and clear all night. Also the way the flesh version of Sasha keeps saying she didn't do it even when I don't ask her to. But I am convinced of her innocence. Just like I believe in reincarnation. You might as well look on the bright side.

'She couldn't have done it,' I say. Pazazu is looking sceptical, though. 'Thing is, Sasha has always been more than one person. Driftwood on the astral tides, she says, schizo say her close friends. She is perfectly capable of not knowing whether she has done it. Or of believing herself totally when she tells me she's innocent.'

I snuff up the aroma of freshly ground Guatemalan coffee which doesn't quite mask the ever-present olfactory echo of Nails's death, another way he is always going to haunt me.

'Why don't you do something to help me?' I say, doing my renowned Oliver Hardy, but Pazazu is still mute and smirking. 'Just tell me who did it, mate. If it's Sasha we will get her a good lawyer. Plead insanity. One look at her collected work and the jury will swallow that.'

'Are you all right?' says the real Sasha, sounding genuinely concerned. I didn't hear her drift in.

'Did you have to do that?' I say, dabbing at the scalding coffee with which I have just customised my army fatigues. Sasha hands me my mail, one postcard inviting me to the opening of an exhibition from someone who has no idea of how much I hate conceptual art. She then tips a small avalanche of parcels and letters on to the table and proceeds to sort through it. Her face glows. She is in demand. But from whom?

Some of the letters are about art but more are requests for photos, used knickers, locks of hair and second-hand items and substances you would think no one would particularly want, stuff we all produce ourselves several times a day. There are long screeds delineating the depths of devotion that her willing slaves would be only too pleased to demonstrate should they ever be granted an audience. These are put to one side just in case our domestic staff quit or, more likely, get the chair for murdering Nails.

'You haven't forgotten about the cable shoot today?' says Sasha.

'You can't be serious.' But she is, she is. The show must go on.

'What have you been doing all night?' she says. 'You can't brood on things. You have to let them go.'

Which is true, if useless.

'We've had a threatening phone call, from someone using a gizmo to alter his voice. Some guy who fancies himself as a Satanic Adept,' I say.

'How do you know it's a guy?' she says, inevitably.

'Satanic covens are generally run by men so that they can initiate gullible young women. Take them under their scaly wings. You know.'

Her eyebrows twitch momentarily as she enjoys some private reference she's not going to share with me. She's wearing her dark blue silk kimono right now but looks anything but homely and domestic. Maybe it's the haunted look in her eyes, or perhaps it's her trademark twitch in her left cheek. Something is up underneath the façade of indifference.

'You coming to the studio with me?' she calls from the bath-room, where she is now cleaning her teeth, loudly and seemingly endlessly, something that has never failed to irritate the fuck out of me. What with one thing and another I had forgotten that we were booked on a live cable show which will be Rob Powers and Sasha Kristinson discussing the return of goddess worship. This might end up as a regular chat show – watch out, Oprah – or a Christmas gift for the Rob Powers fan club or quite possibly evidence for the defence if he ever sues us for the relative harsh-ness of his 'therapy'. Well, if cigarette smokers can claim ignorance of the dangers, what's to stop some disgruntled maso-chist taking his personal therapist to court for cruel and unusual therapy? But we have enough to worry about without projecting negativity into the future, as my old therapist used to say.

I must admit I'm surprised that Sasha wants to go ahead with this. I thought she might decide to be suffering from what some stars call exhaustion, but she is ready at the appointed time. It would take more than murder to come between her and her adoring public.

'You look stunning,' I say, as she returns from her preening mirror. She puckers up her lips and blows me a kiss. A warm, genuine, therefore dazzling smile spreads across her face and stays there. Just to double-check I turn and look out of our window at the crumbling Art Deco skyscrapers. I can see her reflection in the windowpane and the smile is fading slowly and organically and is not switched off immediately, something you see so often in show business.

'How do I look?' she says, her voice much more anxious than when we were discussing the disposal of the body. She is wearing thigh-length silver boots and a shiny red latex outfit underneath an enormous camelhair coat. Her hair is freshly washed and hennaed. She likes blood red, in fact she likes red blood. As I do. But we will get to that later; we have a show to do.

Do I look all right? Who's going to notice next to Supreme Ogress Sasha? My army fatigues and shiny red boots would be nondescript in London but seem to terrify the average New Yorker, who obviously thinks a blazer with brass buttons is the ultimate in style. As long as it cost enough, of course. And the label is both prominent and easily recognisable. And a neat side parting and some preppy tie and ... never mind, let's get on. We are waiting for a cab on the sidewalk right now, not perhaps the best strategy if our killer is lurking nearby, but Sasha just knows we will get one. Ah Sasha! Her lips are gleaming, her eyes are bright and I would love to know why she is so happy.

'You know some people would be upset by ritual murder in their own home,' I say, but before she can answer that a cab arrives just as Sasha said it would. Before we can get in it a male street person of indeterminate age shambles up. As almost always happens, he seems to bond with me immediately however much I try to avoid his eyes, but then something turns him hostile. I give him the look, but he's already had seven shades of shit kicked out of him recently. What does he care?

'She's beautiful,' he says, then a triumphant smile appears as he jabs a gnarled old finger at me. 'But you got a bald head.'

'You can't have everything,' I say and get in.

Now he is leering at us, face pressed up against the window.

It's a distressing spectacle but no worse than the one I see in the mirror when I give the driver directions. I really must get some sleep. And try to drink less coffee. 'Wild-eyed' doesn't quite cut it; 'deranged' is close; perhaps only 'manic' will do.

'Had any bright ideas in the night?' I ask as we set off at a brisk lick leaving our new friend cackling gleefully on the side-walk. 'You know the way discarnate entities appear to you in dreams and offer useful advice? Can we get them to spirit Nails's cadaver away?'

Sasha says nothing, which is also a worrying sign. She's obviously close to cracking up. She nods her head in the direction of the driver, but I'm not worried about security because the cab driver is called Ibrahim and doesn't look like he can speak his own language never mind English. Or whatever it is that Sasha speaks.

She stays silent as we rattle our way over the potholes on the way to the studio, which is someone's house in the Upper Eighties. That someone, John Haskins, is also English, another Northern exile. It was after his initiation into our little coven that he offered Sasha this chat show opportunity, which obviously proves that what punters call black magic works. We are getting our cab fare paid anyway, and I am to be paid a derisory fee to film it.

Suddenly Phil Collins slithers on to the airwaves and it's like trying to eat about ten marshmallows without the chocolate — bland, pointless and ultimately nauseating. Someone, not me, starts to berate the driver in no uncertain terms.

'Turn that fucking shit off! Now!' A harsh voice rasps through my throat and my vision blurs momentarily before normal service is resumed. The music stops and so does the temporary insanity.

'Calm down,' says Sasha, to me. 'What's got into you?'

Maybe the question should be who's got into you?

'You know I hate having to meet Rob,' I say, and although her eyes have rolled upwards into her head I continue: 'I mean, why does not being able to sing or knowing how to tune a guitar qualify you to talk on politics? Or sex? Or anything else?'

Sasha isn't even looking at me now and, what's worse, she's right. It takes a few more blocks of deep breathing and the visualisation of a misty glade before I manage to calm down sufficiently to pay the man and explain what a receipt is.

The doorman rides with us in the elevator, which involves him staring at Sasha's feet the whole time. There's another potential client there, but the man we have come to visit has actually grovelled underneath those shiny silver boots.

John Haskins is fabulously rich but he still can't look us in the eye and looks and sounds like he always does, as if he has been surprised in an act of congress with an underage orangutan. His stutter is worse today, but we all know by now not to complete his sentences for him. He always carries on regardless until he has said whatever we know he is going to say. I just don't feel like it today. I wait patiently while he introduces his new boyfriend who is providing the cable link.

The little munchkin is tanned, worked out and wearing something casual from Gap. I don't know why Haskins didn't just order a blow-up doll from some catalogue.

Rob is wrapped in black leather, as usual. He's such a rebel.

Once I have established what I need to do to operate the camera, I want to be somewhere else but there is no escape. The first condescending nod and smirk from Rob reminds me that I don't like being with him when he is a Rock God rather than a punter. Sasha is spewing out orders like a demented fax machine while Haskins, also wearing Gap and a fresh hair weave, fails to get a word in edgeways, although he manages the start of several.

I leave them to it. Five minutes of blissful seclusion in the bathroom are eventually cut short by Sasha's voice. 'John has something to say to you,' she says.

I recall that I am in no way beholden to Haskins. I don't exactly care if Sasha does any more cable television.

'Tell him to start now and I'll be with him in a minute,' I say, prompting Sasha into a lecture about respecting other people's disabilities.

Back in the room where the interview will be shot, I notice that Rob's right foot is beating a quiet tattoo on the carpeted floor and he is chewing gum furiously. There is a glistening layer of fresh sweat on his face, also spreading across his black T-shirt. Something is sending messages around his wiry body, and there are only two possibilities: he might feel glad to be alive on a fine spring morning such as this, or he might have decided to return to the powders and potions he has already spent three and a half decades in close and careful study.

It's a close call but I think it just might be drugs and that Nails might have been involved somewhere. Which begs the question. 'Where's mine?' I say to Rob as I frame his loathsome face with the camera.

'Excuse me?'

'The toot. Where's mine? Or is it artists only? Did you give Sasha some?'

'I don't do drugs,' she says.

'You actually believe that, don't you?' I say. 'Which is why you are such an accomplished liar. You honestly don't know yourself when you are telling the truth.'

'I step in and out of systems of belief. As and when I need them,' she says. 'Truth is a movable feast.'

'Sounds like that's a good way of saying you're a hypocrite,' says Rob.

Sasha looks like Rob has just tipped a bucket of ice-cold water over her head, but she knows this sort of thing happens whenever he is not strapped to the hot seat in the Chamber. In civilian life submissives are always faux-dominant, whiny, annoying and . . . I no longer care now that Rob forestalls any possible retaliatory action from Sasha by getting out a silver vial, unscrewing the top and depositing a small mound of white powder on the table.

It takes self-control, but we manage not to bang our heads together in the rush of the Gadarene swine towards the table. As Sasha troughs out then launches into the inevitable me-me-me rhapsody, I wonder whether she will get careless and say something about Nails under the influence. But she will be talking about herself for the foreseeable future. Perhaps she will even tell us how she did it.

While the torrent of words flow, Rob is staring at me with a sort of cold triumph in his eyes. He knows the struggle it took to give up. He's knows how much stronger the drug is when you start again. And how humiliating it is going to be for me to give in in front of him.

'You in, too?' says Rob, barely able to stand under the weight of his heavy irony. He keeps fanning the coke out like a croupier playing with a brand-new pack of cards, spreading swaths of beautiful white powder over the glass-topped table. Then we get the 'I've got a platinum American Express card' routine as he paints an inviting cloudscape with what must be several thousand dollars' worth of toot.

There is no point on dwelling on the servile way I have to behave in order to get my line. I'm not proud of it, but I can't just sit here and watch it all disappear before my very eyes. And then have to listen to them jabber incessantly. My eyes look terribly bloodshot as I stoop to the tabletop, but I already know Sasha doesn't care how I look. If she did she would have left years ago. Once it hits the top of everyone's heads we have simultaneous monologue.

'We should make sure it's lit right . . .' begins Rob. But I can't hear him because I'm telling Sasha about why I should be getting paid more for doing this: ' . . . Haskins is loaded. Why do you all believe that bullshit about doing freebies "just to get a foot in the door".'

'... We should have got a limo...' she is telling Haskins, who is still half-way through a sentence he started five minutes ago.

'I want to be shot left profile,' says Rob.

'Like John Lennon?' says Sasha. I try not to think about her obsession with dead rock stars and the day she invited in a group of Japanese Spider Black fans in for tea and a look at the casket photographs. But that's easy because Rob is still talking at me.

'And it's, like, no way do I want to sound like I'm giving orders, but I'm supposed to just publicise some cable station for nothing and not even get lit properly?'

'Rob,' I'm saying simultaneously. 'I've got a "give a fuck" meter here. And the needle's on zero.' And on. And on.

Some time later the snowstorm diminishes down to a frantic blather and it's time to film the interview which will be live on cable to quite possibly more than the four people we have in this room. There will be no editing; whatever we shoot will be broadcast. Sasha will have to phone everyone she has ever met to see what they thought of it when we get back. If they like it, she will be unbearable. If they don't like it, she will be insufferable. I think I'm going out tonight. And I think I know what that five thousand dollars I took off Nails is going to be spent on. Sasha has disappeared briefly but reappears looking frazzled.

'I only ate half a muesli bar today and I just had to throw that up,' she says proudly. Now she thinks she is thinner she is correspondingly more radiant and bewitching.

I already set the shot up but it's hard to resist the urge to wrest the camera from its tripod and lurch about the room trying to make the viewer seasick if I possibly can. Something is certainly working on Sasha's frontal lobes.

'. . . power exchange games are of course rituals which awaken the pagan within us all, setting free the chthonic forces of mother nature which patriarchy has seen fit to repress during the Xtian era, now thankfully coming to a close. Not before time.' says Sasha.

I couldn't agree more, but she wants me to disagree. And it's my cue. I only had one line and I've just about forgotten . . . Ah yes. 'Do you think we could leave out that stuff about the Xtian era?' I say, not having to act the cowardice. 'I mean, the Xtians tend to send letter bombs these days. That turning the other cheek stuff seems to have gone out of fashion.' Sasha glares at me because I have built my part up a little. 'I agree with what you're saying, of course. It's just that . . .'

'You have no balls?' she says icily. 'I'm sorry, viewers. I am surrounded by poodles who wish to mute my awesome power.'

Her eyes flash and I feel a faint echo of that thrill I had the first time I saw her. I still need whatever it is she has got. If only she would stop killing people. I didn't say that. I didn't even think it. Well, who else could have done it? Through the long sleepless night I had plenty of time to go over the events of yesterday. I remember hearing the door slam as she went out, but she could of course have just slammed it and hidden in the flat. There is no shortage of places that a quasi-dwarf might be able to secrete themselves in.

There are the closets where she could hang out among her large collection of leather and rubber overcoats, with her wide selection of battery-driven toys close at hand if she got bored.

There are cages, playpens you can't get out of, and even a coffin lined in red silk which she keeps for a disc jockey who specialises in heavy metal. His formative years must have included the works of Edgar Allan Poe or the films of Roger Corman, for he is never happier than when he is supposedly buried alive. I did the graveyard tape that plays inside the coffin – church bells, the whistling of an eerie wind, the occasional blast of thunder and lightning, torrential rain. It probably would have been more realistic with a bunch of teenagers getting drunk and then desecrating the graves, but he likes it the way it is. I have often toyed with the idea of putting chewing gum over the airholes in the coffin, but I wouldn't want to give him the satisfaction of actually being buried alive. He's such a ghoul; the sort of creepy occult pedant who sports Victorian sideburns and spends every waking hour trying to unearth the one text that will give him the secret key to the eternal mysteries. But the occult is like a soap opera: it never resolves, and once you're hooked you have to keep tuning in.

Then there's . . . this could degenerate into a massive slew of detail which would make confinement enthusiasts slaver and leave everyone else cold, so you will just have to take my word for it. She could easily have hidden in the flat while I went out. But how would she have arranged for a strong man to stand still while she emasculated him? She's very persuasive, but Nails was a man who liked to set his own agenda. And even if, like most dominants, he occasionally liked to see how the other half lives, he wouldn't have willingly kissed goodbye to his pride and joy.

If Sasha had surprised him with one of her many knives . . . She is supposed to use them to define fiery pentagrams to invoke and banish unruly spirits, but they are all sharp enough to have done the deed . . .

Sasha is about to draw breath after a blistering attack on the Pope that will no doubt put her on the Vatican's list of witches. She hopes. 'Rob Powers,' I say, 'perhaps you could explain why you have made a fortune out of other people's deviant sexuality without sharing with the public the details of your own sex life?'

Rob's face crumples momentarily before the iron man of Noo Yawk rock'n'roll persona returns.

'Just roll the film, man,' he says with a dismissive wave of the hand. 'Nobody cares what you think.'

He nods to himself while I burn up with rage, which lasts all the way through a statement from Sasha about female eroticism, which lasts something like the length of the Stone Age. When there is eventually a pause I have to wipe the smile off Rob's face. I just have to.

'It's like . . . Well, we all know the theory of female domination, don't we?' I say clumsily, but my heart is beating twice as fast as usual. And Rob's smile widens as he sees I am angry.

'What about the practice?' I say. 'Why don't you show us some of your scars, Rob?'

Nobody except us has seen the white whip welts that never healed properly, which is odd considering the countercultural credibility they would give him. I make sure Rob's face fills the screen. He likes the occasional tease from Sasha about his proclivities, but he doesn't like this. Not on live television. Absolutely not. He actually does flap his mouth without managing to say anything. I zoom in to an invasive close-up of his eyes while my heart beats with a savage joy. Whatever he does in the future, however rich he gets, I will always have this moment. Rob Powers, twitching and wriggling on the hook, live on cable. If he were a salmon I would get one of those clubs and give him a sound pounding right now. But maybe not – it's fun watching him approach his first long-overdue heart attack.

'Well, why don't we talk about you?' he says, pointing straight at the camera. 'What do you get from living with a female dominatrix?'

'I am not a client. Unlike you,' I say.

'Maybe. But you don't seem to be answering my question, and I am sure many people would be interested to know what is the division of labour in this household. Are you her "manager"? Or are you one of those geeks in aprons who beg to do the washing up? One of the ones who can't even get it up. One of the ones who don't even want to get it up.'

He steeples his fingers and inclines his head as he looks at the camera gravely. I should feel in control. I have the camera, no one can see me, but he has won again. Somehow. It's what comes of being famous, I suppose. Or is it just because the bastard is taller and better endowed than me? Have we really come no further than that in several millennia of evolution? Not really. I have standard tackle – well, apart from the rings and things, the brands, the home-made tattoo of the Tyr rune on the underside of the shaft and . . . well, never mind about that. Let's not get swamped with details again.

As it's better to give the opposition enough rope to hang themselves, not always a figure of speech in Rob's case, I don't respond to his last effort.

'Let's face it,' he says. 'You're just pissed because I'm successful and you're not.'

He is practically doing a lap of honour round the studio right now and Sasha is looking at me, one eyebrow tilted as if to ask: Are you going to let him say that?

Seconds tick by. As this is live television I am not entirely sure what we should do. It's a situation calling for great tact and sensitivity and the judgement of Solomon. I put the camera back on the tripod and walk over to where Rob is still grinning at me. Before I can retract my boot to aim it right at his nuts or the Mulhadra Chakra as Sasha would have it, he backs down to the extent of holding out two hands, palms extended towards me. I stand there glowering like the Neanderthal he always reduces me to and then the show goes on. I scowl at the camera as I pass it and wonder whether I should have unveiled myself. Still, it is unlikely that anyone is watching this, never mind the handful of people who wish to grind my bones to dust. Sasha talks about male violence long enough to prove she knows absolutely nothing about it until Rob feels it's safe to rattle my cage again.

'. . . like when you get too close to exposing the truth,' he says with a significant glance at me.

'One more word out of you and we will show a video of you in harness,' I say.

'Which you probably get your kicks out of whenever I'm not there.'

'OK,' I say, walking over close enough for him to get a blast of my coffee breath. 'Like countless others I enjoy consensual sadomasochism with a regular partner and this is still supposed to be daring or something at the end of the twentieth century. While it's OK to own a gun, beat someone's brains out in a boxing-ring, or listen to your drab dull music, the depiction of consensual s/m is too much for governments to handle just about anywhere in the world.'

Rob has started to slow handclap me and Sasha looks like she could spontaneously combust right now, but I will not be silenced.

'So, unfashionable and indeed illegal as it may be, I am on occasion, on request, the dominant half of this relationship.'

I shouldn't have said it but it was the thing about doing the washing up. I never do the washing up. I don't. I never have and I never will.

The air in the room is frozen and it may be that I have finally achieved what many occultists strive for: I have frozen time. Sasha holds a hand up to silence me. Seeing that Rob's face is sneer-free for the moment, I manage to shut up.

'Well, that wasn't in the script, viewers,' says Sasha glacially, 'but as we are breaking the fourth wall today, let's define terms for those who wish to know more about the fastest-growing way to sexual fulfilment. We all know s/m is a continuum, a pendulum which swings between the two opposite poles, sometimes stopping along the way as the participants define and redefine themselves. Although it is much more than a master–slave relationship in many power exchange relationships, the slave submits and by doing so controls the master. The Bottom may acquiesce to the Top, but they both need each other equally. It's not about abuse of anyone's rights, it's about shining some light on those dark parts of yourself that the government and the Church and Mom and Dad don't want you to know about. Once you have escaped the endless tedium of vanilla sex you are free to realise your dreams. But remember. Let's be careful out there.'

She holds a winning smile, and I can see she has timed this statement to bring our segment of the public-access cable show to a triumphant conclusion. I nod to Haskins's boyfriend to cue the video of Sasha's live performance, and we can all relax.

The ensuing argument lasts all the way home until I put on headphones, shades and a latex hood to declare the issue closed. It won't be the last I've heard of it, but calls keep stacking up on our various answerphone systems through the evening and there is plenty of e-mail for Sasha to chip her nailvarnish on. I decide to do something really transgressive to try to escape the humiliation of the day – I watch about three episodes of *Are You Being Served* and an *Inspector Morse*.

Watching the white-haired old clown drink a pint of beer nearly has me in tears for the country I loathed while I was actually living there. Sasha suddenly manifests in the middle of my wake for merrie olde England. Her eyes are big and sparkly, the way they always were when we first met. She has joyous tidings to relate.

'MTV want to run the clip on their news.'

'News?' I say, but then I remember that they were always

running features on bands whose careers wouldn't last as long as our supply of coffee filters. 'What do they want?'

'You and Rob arguing. And little old *moi*, of course. Think of the publicity. Worldwide exposure. Will you sign a release?'

'Yes. Will Rob?'

She comes over all coy all of a sudden.

'Of course. He would do anything I say,' she says.

Just like the rest of us, I think. She scampers off and I wonder if she will ever grow up. Or whether she will ever trade me in for a younger, sleeker model. Or whether she already has traded me in and that guy killed Nails. Or whether it would be for a woman and . . . it's time to spend another productive half-hour trying to stop my hands shaking.

4

Easter Saturday Night

THERE IS ANOTHER answerphone message.

'By now you will have become aware of my powers. I am still observing your activities. I was prepared to allow the selling of bogus talismans or the marketing of the sexual services of your "Scarlet Woman", in reality a whore masquerading as an artist. When you choose to distort my message to make yourself appear an Adept I am forced to take action. The butchering of the degenerate drug dealer is just the start. I might have known you do not have the courage to contact the forces of law and order. You can rest assured that I will not either. For I am your judge and jury. I have weighed you in the scales of justice and found you wanting. Part of your punishment is to wait in fear before it is carried out. You may be able to flee to another country, and live once more from the profits of the whore you live with. Rest assured, wherever you run I will track you down. You will hear from me again.'

'What's wrong?' says Sasha, already wound up from hauling Nails's body out of the freezer. I am still coping with this fresh input. How could he know this stuff? Sasha would probably say: Why do you think it's a he? I haven't got round to telling her about our Satanic phone freak's latest message, but it wouldn't be useful information for her to have right now. And we really must get ready for our guests.

But after a neutron bomb like that I can't cope. It's someone close. Someone who can see and hear what is going on inside the flat. Which means the neighbours or Sasha herself who might manage something like this. She can be a bit of a prankster at times: cutting off the air supply in a restraint scenario for instance is one of her favourites.

Then there's the guy upstairs with his horror film fetish. Maybe our missing kitchen slaves could have killed Nails but they are professional victims rather than predators. The other explanation is that someone can travel astrally, but I don't really believe all that stuff. Our clients do, though, and it's time to get ready.

Planning a Satanic initiation is just as tough as preparing for any other dinner party. But soon there are more ticks than spaces on my checklist. The ritual space has been cleansed, the daggers have been polished, Nails is freshly thawed and securely butt-plugged to keep his insides inside him – there are some manifestations you can do without in black magic – the chalices have been washed and dried and the red wine has been uncorked and left to breathe. Added to which I have to look up which constellations the planets are in and write that down in sperm, spittle and blood on black paper. Although many on the left-hand path don't hold with astrology, I like a bit of tradition; it gives us something to hold on to in an ever-changing world.

After I have done that you can't make out the words, just like a Rob Powers performance, come to think of it, so I add some white ink and – hey presto! – we have an amusing and evocative

placemat that sets the tone for the whole evening. It may seem
unnecessarily time-consuming, but this process serves the
purpose of enabling us to feel superior to the paying customers,
which is very important in show business.

Magical masturbation is, of course, hard work and not
indulged in merely for the purposes of sensual pleasure. Oh no.
I had to concentrate hard to visualise a successful conclusion to
this evening's little soirée and also to request from whomever
might be listening that the name of the murderer be revealed to
us before long.

'We need to know now!' said my glamorous assistant. But you
can't push any harder that that. You just have to wait and see.

As for the blood, as with any addiction, once you start it's
hard to stop. Sasha and I both keep a small silver vial of our
freshest gore secreted about our persons. It's the claret of the
gods, nothing quite like it once you have got the taste. It keeps
our scarifications fresh and vibrant, at the cutting edge you might
say. It is also a useful distancing device on a boring social occasion
to unscrew the top and take a quick nip now and then . . . not
that ennui is likely to be a problem tonight.

Perhaps after Sasha has waved her magic wand often enough
Nails will consent to join us, although if the spirit Nails is
anything like the corporeal one used to be he will probably show
up about two days late wondering why everyone's pissed off with
him. White people, they're just so uptight.

As usual I am anything but cool as I contemplate all the
things that could go wrong tonight. We already have two cancel-
lations due to pressure of work, or perhaps the malign influence
of Saturn, depending on how you look at it. That just leaves us
with Rob and JC. But they are both paying customers so the
show must go on.

Now Nails/Osiris has thawed he is starting to become about

as fragrant as a roadie who has a part-time gig as a mortician. Sasha catches my eye.

'Incense,' we both say at once, a delightful couple-type moment.

When we have set every oil burner in the house going and set up candles in the ornamental skulls, and polished the real one to a deathly shine, we have to come to a decision about using Nails as a prop. Is it really such a good idea?

'Rob is already docile, but this is a way of enslaving JC for ever,' says Sasha. 'We get him to dump the body and then we can get him to take the rap if it all goes wrong.'

That seems a very well-worked-out theory. It's obvious she has put a great deal of thought into this little project, which reminds me that she is also clever enough, and mad enough, to have snuffed Nails out. I look at her for a very long time but I get it all back and more. My usual voodoo isn't going to work tonight. She isn't for all practical purposes my little Sasha any more.

'Isn't it just a little bit risky?' I say. 'Like if Rob or JC turns into a born-again Xtian one day and goes straight to the police?'

She broods on that for a while, her brow darkening sufficiently for me to dread what arcane occult wisdom is going to issue forth from her blood-reddened lips.

'You can't make an omelette without breaking eggs,' she says finally.

My thin veneer of rationality starts to crack. 'It's a pointless risk, it's . . .' I'm reduced to waving my hands about like your average Italian American.

'Calm down,' she says. 'We are going to enact the rite of the raising of Osiris. We are going to make him whole again.'

'Which will do what?' I say, tired of making jokes now it

appears that Sasha actually is Nyx or Kali or, even scarier, Camille Paglia.

'It will scare the shit out of them so we get their money. Plus we get to find out if Rob could have done Nails. This is modern-day necromancy. We bring the dead back to life and they lead us to the truth.'

'He was on live radio,' I say slowly and firmly. 'I heard the broadcast. I've already told you this,' I say in that special voice I reserve for things I've already told her. She gives me a look that just about pinions me to the wall behind me. Once it's been settled that that was not an appropriate tone of voice, we move on.

'He's looked better,' I say, after a glance at Nails. 'Funny, he was always going on about Egypt. You know, how he was probably descended from some top deity of the time. Now's his chance to prove it. Incidentally, where's his Johnson? Or have you had it stuffed and mounted?'

Sasha's lips twitch slightly but she spares me whatever went through her mind right then. Instead she clambers up on to the table and reaches for a bottle of chilli vodka from the top shelf.

'Alas, poor Nails. I knew him well,' I say, gagging slightly. 'Wasn't the dick eaten by a bird originally and not steeped in chilli vodka?'

'We must create our own myths to suit our contemporary circumstances,' she says, back in schoolmarm mode. One foot wrong and I could be hearing why the last two thousand years are a Xtian male conspiracy against the goddess and her represent-atives on earth, most specifically Sasha Kristinson. All of which is true; I just don't want to hear it. Again. I suddenly have the urge to do something really transgressive, like put some baseball on the television or insist that Celine Dion is my favourite recording artiste or, hush my mouth, book two front-row seats for *Cats*.

Rob arrives and is immediately given a severe dressing-down by Sasha for having no cocaine. Eventually she storms off to stick more pins in Rob's effigy, leaving me to play host.

'You work out,' says Rob, looking at the dumbbells I pick up now and again.

'Yes, but the weights are next to the couch,' I say. 'And the remote control.'

'But you like to fight.'

'Oh yes.'

'I've got a gig for you,' he says, while we stare intently at some thinly clad black female rumps on MTV. They gyrate slowly and lewdly, but we hate each other too much to make any comment. 'I need a bodyguard,' he says. 'I keep getting this hate mail.'

I know. I keep sending it. He must be terrified. There's nothing like some ancient black magic curses written in real blood to get people's attention.

'I'm serious. I've been offered a spoken word tour. I want Sasha to support. And I want you along. It would be more like tour managing. Doing the sound. Carrying my supplies.' He taps his nose to underline the cocaine reference.

'But I have given up,' I say.

'Like this afternoon? If you did give up you won't be tempted to stick your snout in the trough.'

Just when I have managed to get clean. As he well knows. He would, of course, love me to start again; they love to spread their sickness around. And it wouldn't be long before 'they' becomes 'we' again?

'There's some European dates. England too. You interested?'

'Maybe.'

Maybe? I long for a cup of stewed tea in the Walworth Road

in a chipped cup. I want to wait for a red bus in the rain. I want people working in service industries to be pointlessly rude to me. I want to eat a bacon sandwich on white bread with enough English mustard to make my sinuses sting. God forgive me, but I want to see Richard and Judy again, especially in another five years. Let's see him keep smiling then . . .

Most of all I want to see if I'm wanted for that killing which I think was manslaughter anyway, although it's maybe pushing the envelope of self-defence to jump up and down on someone's head when they are already unconscious. As far as I was concerned it was just a lap of honour. I didn't really . . . well, I probably did want to kill him if you are going to be all judgemental about it. The drag is I can't tell anyone.

I have done what Arnold Schwarzenegger and all the rest of them can only dream about and I can't tell anyone. Sasha knows, but it's starting to work against me now. Like if I don't worship her utterly she might turn me in. Not that she ever would. Would she?

Rob is still smirking at me, enjoying the power he wields in his world. Which is a reminder that we should be in mine again.

'You're just trying to split us up again,' I say. 'Anyway, if it's your poetry you won't need bodyguards. Who's going to be there?'

'Always bitter,' says Rob, a grin stretching his haggard jowls. 'Just ignore the little green-eyed monster.'

I try to remain impassive while he grins at me. Luckily JC arrives before I concede any more ground.

We didn't stipulate a dress code over the phone so he has come as himself: jeans, denim jacket, a Yankees baseball cap with an 'I sobered up for this shit?' button on it.

Sasha serves them drinks – chilli vodka cocktails, needless to say – and then starts to harass the help. It doesn't take long for me to get tired of that, so I suggest we let the guests chatter away among themselves for a while. As we leave our guests to mingle, Sasha has a conspiratorial giggle for me to share.

'Is that the same chilli vodka that . . .?' I can barely say it.

'Why not? It's just like communion wine really. This is my body. This is my blood.' She gives me an impish smile.

'I hope they burn you alive,' I say, with more feeling that I had bargained for.

'Steady,' she says. 'It's too early to be regressing to your past lives.'

She is convinced that I once had her burned at the stake. I'm beginning to think she may be right, but she got her sums wrong. It's her that gets *me* burned at the stake this time round. But it doesn't do to dwell on that. We rejoin the guests.

'I walked past Katz's deli to get here,' says Rob, taking centre stage like he always does. 'It reminded me of *When Harry Met Sally*. The fake orgasm scene.'

Sasha gives us all a skewed smile. As the only initiate into the feminine mysteries present, she is the only one capable of rending the veil for us. As she never tires of reminding us.

We await her answer with some trepidation as we are all aware that it's just possible that on occasion we may have been the victims of a deception.

'A powerful ritual preserved on film for the moronic masses,' she acknowledges. 'Serving to remind the dumber sex that they will never really know what's going on.'

Rob is staring respectfully at the floor near Sasha's feet, too servile even to set eyes on her shiny silver boots. JC is trying to smirk but can't. Most sex for JC starts with a financial transaction, so much so that he probably gets a hard on when he opens his wallet these days. But that doesn't alter the fact that Sasha's words are like red-hot skewers dipped in some especially powerful and pungent Tiger Balm and then dug slowly underneath my fingernails. And she is about to stick more of them into those tender regions we like to keep well hidden from the light of day.

'You can never possess the almighty power of female sexuality,' she says. Which is not exactly news to the three stooges standing opposite her. 'It is a force beyond the control of mere men.'

'And yet a small ritual offering of a tub of Ben and Jerry's will melt even the flintiest heart,' I say. Well, somebody's got to say something.

'Indeed,' she says. 'Speaking of offerings. Did we all bring something for the Dark Goddess?'

JC displays a jar with a frightened-looking hamster in it. He knows he is not supposed to do that, so he gives us the look and bares some of his off-white teeth in a sneer. 'A blood sacrifice always works,' he says, his right hand jabbing at us karate-style as he tries to get the point across. 'We are higher life forms. Who cares about dumb animals?'

'You will pay dearly for that,' says Sasha, and she licks her lips once more. 'No doubt that was your motivation,' she says. 'Like you didn't know that we do not harm living creatures here.'

I raise an eyebrow at that, but she is busy replenishing her chalice.

'You don't need dumb animals for a blood sacrifice,' I say. 'You can sacrifice something that you honour more than even human life.'

I take the admission money from the silver collection plate and light a match. Now I have everyone's attention. 'You don't need to sacrifice the first-born,' I say. 'You would be surprised how far you can get with inanimate objects.'

'Mathew!' screeches Sasha. I turn round and see that she is totally distraught. I have genuinely shocked her, something I have been trying to do for years. 'Put those bills down!' she says.

There is a mad glitter in her eyes and I don't like the way she is holding her ritual dagger, so I blow out the match. 'Can't you take a joke?' I say, but her look says that there are some things which actually are sacred.

There is no doubt that she has been exhibiting an extra layer of manic intensity since the murder, all of which tends to exacerbate my suspicions regarding her involvement. But as I don't have a ducking stool handy I will have to bide my time. Maybe the truth will out later on as the hallucinogenics take hold. There's nothing like a fistful of mushrooms, a bottle of brandy and a few joints to stimulate a good old heart to heart.

Sasha claps her hands together and insists that we move into the Chamber. I lead the way, anxious to see JC under the whip. When we are all there we kill the lights and let the candles flicker. We take a moment to acknowledge the new atmosphere before proceeding. Eventually we look at Sasha. In here she has to be in charge.

'You must first be scourged, JC,' she says briskly, without any unseemly sexual resonance. But there is still a sweaty leer on JC's fat face.

'I got tattoos all over my body,' he rasps. 'How much worse do you think you can be, little lady?' The tone is dismissive, contemptuous even. Sasha's face remains calm, but I know he has booked himself some scar tissue.

'I should have known you would be a pig for it,' she says, stepping on the word pig a little harder than she needed to. JC doesn't seem to mind. Indeed, he is shucking off his foul-smelling denim shirt to reveal a carcass covered with some expensive but crude tattoos: big-breasted women on Harley Davidsons, the names of long-gone Heavy Metal bands, a Ninja warrior, and Satan himself with his little red pitchfork. No one can think of anything to say to that little lot, but there is never any danger of silence developing when Sasha is about.

'You may be familiar with the theory that the submissive is really in charge in a power exchange relationship,' she says. 'It's become something of a cliché as s/m tries to define its space in the contemporary sexual market-place. We don't work like that here. I'm in charge. I decide when you have had enough. There are no safe words. You have no option other than to remain in the cuffs until the scourging is completed. You may beg for mercy, but you will be for ever a probationer if you do so.'

I wink at JC, who is not so beery and bold now that he has realised that this initiation is going to involve more than a Chinese burn and learning a few secret passwords. Sasha's voice becomes more portentous once she has cuffed his arms above his head to a steel flogging post.

'The only way for you truly to cast off the shackles of your past identity and forge a new one is with a cleansing baptism of fire.'

Right on cue, with the last word she swung her arm and let the lash cut his back. Any commercially available erotica will probably suggest that a whipping can be borne by a fit young man with nothing more than mounting sexual excitement to show for it. As the first stroke lacerates his flesh, JC's head wrenches backwards and his mouth opens to its fullest extent. It is obviously more than he had bargained for, but he can't actually say that.

'Is that the best you can do, you little mutant?' he says.

Sasha applies one clothes peg to each nipple then stands back and starts again. The next lash catches him higher up, somewhere else where there is no erotic stimulus to dim the pain. It's probably very therapeutic for Sasha but it's not doing JC much good as the lashes accumulate. When it's done JC manages a rueful smile. 'Boy, am I glad I never got my back tattooed,' he gasps, surmising accurately that some of those wounds will never heal. Sasha is walking on air because she enjoys the chance to express herself and not just do what the clients want. I feel a little light-headed myself as the mushrooms come on.

'Isn't that the last of Nails's stuff?' says Sasha, as I hand her a spliff.

'Yeah, smoke this in remembrance of me.'

Before we can get any further with our Bible class the grass takes hold and I suddenly need to be a long way away from all this. Dope brings back the teenage hippie in me who wants to know whether it isn't, you know, a bit heavy playing around with dead bodies for money, but the show must go on. And it's time for the entrance of the star.

In the olden days ventriloquism was used to convince the punters that the dead had risen; the magus/witch/wise person would intone a few words looking at the relevant corpse in near-darkness, and if no one saw their lips move the punters would be satisfied: they had raised the dead. It's not going to be so easy tonight, but once I have wheeled the freezer containing Nails into the Chamber we have a respectful silence even though they can't see him yet.

Then I get to play a long note on a Tibetan bone trumpet made from a human head to mark the start of the proceedings. Like many another trumpeter, my lips fail me just when I need them most and the note comes out as a strangled fart, but what could be more appropriate for a spot of necromancy than a ghostly death rattle? Especially now the mushrooms are working. The shapes of the faces around the table liquefy and re-form. Sparks tingle up and down my body. We have entered the realm.

For a moment I am convinced that Rob must have been my father at some point in the dim and distant past, but I shrug that off and get back to work. I stand up, all too conscious of some unpleasant chafing from the ligature I just wrapped round my neck. If I tighten it I can impede the flow of blood to my brain, thereby increasing divinatory and erectile capacity. Too much and it's going to be me in the freezer, but as Sasha says, You can't make an omelette without breaking eggs.

'Is the music prepared?' she asks, too imperiously for my liking, but she's Method acting right now. Soon she will actually be the Goddess, and you have to warm up for such things.

'Yes.'

'Very well. Let the rite commence.'

I hit the play button and Ligeti's *Lux Aeterna* cranks into action. Weeping, wailing voices cast adrift in an unsympathetic universe begin to bemoan their fate. Although JC probably recognises the music from *2001* he is still more afraid of anything without a tune or a beat than he is of anything Sasha will do in the name of Satan.

Sasha dims the lights then issues the command to strip. I have already prepared myself for the grim revelation that JC will be more handsomely endowed than I am but I'm glad to report that we are equals.

When the men are all sky clad and Sasha is wearing only a translucent purple gown, we hunker down inside a circle defined by lit candles and let Sasha cleanse the ritual space.

There is always a chance that someone might giggle during the Enochian keys, but on this occasion we have decided that, as we have a freshly slain cadaver, there is no need to summon up the Old Ones. They are probably already here, tapping their feet impatiently and eager to join the fray. At a nod from Sasha I activate some more sound sources, a couple of radios, an old television and some techno that is surprisingly palatable when competing with white noise, a cowboy movie, Alistair Cooke's *Letter from America*, Mahler five and Ligeti's lost souls still vainly seeking salvation in the void.

It's time for number one on our hymn sheet.

'Io Ceruunnos! Io Pan! Io Mercury! Io Mars!' Sasha is putting a lot into this, and I'm glad she has invoked Mercury, the god of communication, healing and trickery, as I am of the opinion that we may fail to raise Nails from the dead. I only hope our sleight of hand is going to be swift enough to pacify our audience. With some difficulty we answer in a ragged unison, trying to match Sasha's manic fervour.

'Io Freya! Io Lilith! Pluto! Lord of the Underworld. Bring your faithful servant back to life.'

We hand round instruments. Soon Rob is drumming away with everything he has got, JC is strumming away on a lyre, and I am whirling a football rattle around my head while summoning up my deepest and most gut-wrenching groans.

Sasha has both arms extended above her head, her breasts prominent under the thin silk of her purple gown as she rattles the ceiling with her caterwauling. Five minutes of this and things actually do feel different.

'We have the carcass of one such dumb animal here in this flat,' screeches Sasha. 'Proof of what happens to those who would seek to betray us. All those who betray the pact shall die!'

Such statements would normally be risky, but no one is going to crack wise as Sasha flings open the freezer and the grim stench of death heads straight for the part of our brain where our ancestors' memories of the smell of a decomposing corpse are stored. Visually, Nails also leaves something to be desired, drained of most of his blood and his mouth frozen open in a silent scream. Holding my breath, I lay him on the floor.

Ligeti's dissonant voices drone on, just about uppermost in the mix, while Sasha rants on. She's good at this. I just hope I'm still her agent when she's fifty and making a good living as a television evangelist. Somehow I remember that magick depends on diamond-hard concentration and shut my brain off to let the Wild Hunt ride.

Just as I can hear the thundering of the horses' hooves and the howls of the pack in full cry, Strauss's *Blue Danube* starts up – I forgot to programme the CD to repeat, and as Strauss comes next on the *2001* soundtrack we are now stuck with the ambience of nineteenth-century Vienna.

I open my eyes and shrug at Sasha, who is glaring at me. Well, she can stamp her little foot and wave her magic dagger all she likes, there will be no more conjurations tonight. Nails will never be reunited with his pride and joy and Osiris will never be made whole again.

Which is a shame. After all the work we put in.

Sasha explains feebly that Nails isn't coming out to play tonight and instead Rob is going to oblige us by deconstructing the concept of death. He doesn't want to, but we are not going to let a little thing like that stand in our way. His vast wealth may be a factor in his selection for this terrible ordeal or it may not. I'll let you decide.

We rub his body with some herbs, among which are deadly nightshade and something that must remain as anonymous as the secret ingredient in Coca-Cola. He is bleating that he took a tab of acid and it's already coming on, but we are not going to be diverted from our path. Sasha puts him in one of his tight latex bodysuits, topped off with a fetching little hood. In the dark, once he has started to lose the outlines of his body he is guaranteed a mystical experience anyway even without the acid.

'May I ask why, Mistress?' he says.

'You will never fear death ever again,' she says. 'And when you return from your journey into the underworld you will be more alive than you have ever been before. Let's get your cuffs on.' She slathers his wrists in Vaseline then cuffs him. Rob looks at JC and then at me and seems to sense that there is no way round this. He climbs in to the freezer.

'Like a lamb to the slaughter,' says Sasha, clicking it shut. She catches my eye. This really is a bit risky even if Rob is a veteran of countless confinement situations and has had every hallucinogenic ever invented.

'There is plenty of air coming through the airholes, Rob,' says Sasha. 'Just breathe deeply and go on your journey. On your return you will have many things to tell us.'

And in the meantime there is the red wine, the guacamole dip and the blue corn tortilla chips for the rest of us.

'You know what would really gross him out?' says Sasha. 'What if we tipped Nails into the freezer with him?'

'Just as the acid took hold,' says JC approvingly.

I laugh politely, to try to smother this puppy before it grows up to be a great rabid slavering hound that will devour us all.

'He would know who killed Nails,' says Sasha, the wine speaking to her very clearly now. 'He's in an altered state, right? He would channel the name of the killer. If we all concentrated hard enough.'

Silence seems to be the best response to that, but as soon as JC picks up that I really don't want it to happen he sides with Sasha. And as soon as she realises that this is a chance to fight back against the hated oppressor, my fate is sealed. Sasha knocks on the freezer lid.

'Got a visitor for you,' she says, giggling immoderately.

As soon as the body flops down on top of Rob she closes the lid and flips the catches once more. It starts to rock as JC and Sasha keep on screeching with laughter and I try not to think about disembowelling JC now he has found a way to make Sasha laugh. Just then there is an almighty hammering at the front door. Sasha and I look at each other. This is it. The cops. The end.

'So you invoked something then,' I say to Sasha. 'Finally. Never thought you had it in you.'

The hammering continues, long and loud enough to signal that they aren't going away.

'You told someone,' I say to JC who already has his jeans on and is presently covering his bloated belly with an Iron Maiden road crew T-shirt.

'No way,' he says. 'I'm going to tell someone? You nuts?'

I pick the ritual knife from the altar, prompting a squeal of protest from Sasha as it's meant to be only for keeping demons at bay.

'Don't leave the protection of the ritual space!' calls Sasha. 'I didn't cleanse the hall.'

'The show's over,' I say, a little coldly perhaps, but when you start to believe your own sales pitch it's time to take a long holiday. My body is not rent apart as I approach the door very quietly, but peering through the spyhole brings me face to face with two unearthly apparitions. Waiting outside are a couple in late middle age. He is wearing golf trousers and an anorak, and she is wearing nothing I ever want to think about ever again. They are both fat and have white hair.

'Didn't you ring to say we were coming?' says the man and bunches his fist to pound on the door once more. As he does that I return to the Chamber to tell them that Sasha's parents are here.

'It's your parents,' I say.

It's not easy for a bleached-out moonchild like Sasha to turn white, but I can now see even more of her already-prominent cheekbones. I'm not sure if she hasn't actually shrunk. She might as well be seven years old right now. After both her pet guinea-pigs have died.

'And I thought they were in Michigan,' I say, thinking that one of the great things about our bohemian lifestyle is that we never see our folks. I was away for last year's visit, but I was confidently expecting Sasha to make a recovery any day now.

It was once fashionable to call the older generation Nazis. As Sasha's German father once marched through Poland in an earlier attempt to unite Europe, this is no modish exaggeration. He then spied for the Americans in postwar Vienna before marrying a local girl and emigrating to America to become a staunch Republican. Sasha's mother was a convent girl who never kicked the habit. She rarely reads a book except the Bible. As far as I know they are unaware of Sasha's artistic career, believing her to be some sort of an actress, which is true enough in its way.

Muffled sounds of turmoil come from within the freezer.

'Are you sure he's going to be all right?' I say.

'There's plenty of air for him to breathe,' she says.

'Well, I suppose he's in the right place if he dies from fright,' I say. 'We could dump the two of them at the same time.'

'Can you baby-sit Rob for five minutes?' says Sasha to JC. He agrees, taking a bottle of whisky and a spliff with him.

'Funny that. You invoke Beelzebub and his host of demons and your dad turns up,' I tell Sasha.

'I told you I was the devil's daughter,' she says, smiling in an especially winning way, blood-red lipstick gleaming in the candlelight. Which is all very well. They are still pounding on the door. 'We lock the door to the Chamber and everything will be all right. We tell them we are going out or something,' says Sasha. I'm convinced. Totally. The hammering continues.

'Shall I let them in, darling?' I say, unscrewing my nipple clamps.

'No, I'll do it,' she says, locking the Chamber and pocketing the key. I watch closely as she approaches the door. She seems to shrink, and I'm not sure I don't actually hear her simper as she opens it.

'Sweetie Pie!' says Momma.

'Surprise!' says Poppa.

'It certainly is,' I say, taking his proffered hand rather than shattering his kneecap with one well-placed boot.

'Hi, Mom. Hi, Dad,' says Sasha.

'Tea anyone?' I say, becoming inexplicably English as Sasha reverts back to her own childhood.

'Tea would be fine,' says Momma, which at least gives me something to do.

'What's that terrible smell?' says Papa.

'The drains,' says his dutiful daughter, lighting yet another incense stick. 'The city has a problem right now.'

'Sheez,' says Papa. 'It smells like someone's died in here. What's in this room?' He rattles the handle of the door to the Chamber as if he's throttling some small sharp-toothed pest.

'It's a dead body and we have a roadie to stay,' says Sasha rather brattishly. 'I don't know which one smells worse.'

She has somehow become an irritating adolescent but nothing is going to alter the cut of Papa's bright yellow check trousers. Neither does it show in his big meatloaf face.

'Do you need to lock your Häagen-Dazs away from Mathew?' he says, chuckling genially.

I watch Sasha seethe, trying to imagine the slow drip effect of that cheery chuckle over a couple of decades.

'I don't eat ice-cream,' says Sasha, as though he should have been able to have perceived this telepathically. 'I'm on a non-dairy diet.'

'No wonder you look so ill. Milk is full of goodness,' says

Mom, who is carrying two extra stones of goodness around with her. Sasha's eyes close momentarily while she swallows her reply to that. It's strange how quickly she has changed from Dark Goddess to their daughter, the person she came here to get away from.

'Look, we just dropped by because we couldn't get tickets for *Cats*. Perhaps we could meet on Easter Monday. See the Easter Parade perhaps?'

She looks old and deflated and worried about never seeing her children again. I wonder whether Sasha's account of her childhood can have been true. I keep forgetting she is an artist, she makes things up. All the time.

'What are we doing on Monday?' says Sasha.

'Better check,' I say, fishing out my mini-filofax and flipping through the pristine pages of the diary section.

'You need snow blinkers to look at this thing,' I say, under the impression I am joking. It quite often gets a laugh from the career obsessives we are usually talking to. But it doesn't really play in the little bit of Michigan we now have in our front room.

'Sasha has another cable broadcast,' I say, having channelled an urgent communication from my own personal goddess. 'Like the one we did today.'

'Yeah, Momma, they're going to use a clip on MTV,' she says, still desperately trying to impress and melting my heart in the process. Papa looks like he is going to pretend not to have heard of MTV but then decides it's better just to grunt his disapproval.

'And we are meeting clients at the Knitting Factory. We have to go there right now,' she says eagerly. 'You know, where they play the really loud, out jazz.'

Probably the word jazz would have sufficed on its own. All of a sudden they want to be somewhere else and who can blame them?

'That's OK honey. We just thought because we couldn't get tickets to the show . . . We did call this afternoon. Guess you're too busy to listen to your messages. We'll catch up with you another time.'

They know she's lying but manage not to say so during an uncomfortable half an hour during which we learn about the weather in the Midwest and what Sasha's brothers and sisters are doing. I can't help noticing that her father looks oddly appropriate perched next to Pazazu as he scans the room looking for clues as to what his daughter is getting up to these days. Eventually, they fall for Sasha's story about an urgent appointment and they are soon gone. Or at least they are now exchanging tearful goodbyes outside the front door.

'Goodbye, Mom. Safe journey, Dad.'

Big hug, sloppy kiss maybe. I don't know as already I have the mouse scurrying about its mat to check my e-mail while my right hand is using the remote to flick through the available television programmes. I want oblivion and I want it now.

'Goodbye, Little Miss Slurpie,' says Mr Kristinson out in the hall. There is that fond chuckle in his voice again as he reels off this no doubt once appropriate family nickname. I could just see Sasha as a winsome pre-teen demanding a Slurpie on each and every visit to the Seven-Eleven. It was probably the highlight of her day back then.

My lips twitch momentarily before returning to the usual grim rictus with which I favour anyone entering my airspace. Sasha totters back into the flat and reaches the bathroom just in time to spend the next fifteen minutes throwing up. She pauses only to repel my offers of help with some screeched obscenities and then finally appears looking like Dracula's grandmother.

'Sorry,' she says, very quietly for once.

'What was that?' I say. 'Homage to Diamanda Galas?'

'One of the freaks used to call me Little Miss Slurpie on the net.'

It takes a moment for it to hit me.

Sasha used to trawl the net having deviant cybersex, recording the results on her laptop then publishing it in arty little magazines, exhibiting it in galleries or singing the results with obscure pop groups. I used to have to set them to music until I insisted that we had no future as a couple unless we separated our personal and professional lives. As she looks like she may never speak again, I might as well say it.

'It doesn't mean your Dad was one of the freaks: It could be a coincidence.'

'There was this creepy look in his eye. He's changed. He doesn't smile any more. Just stares straight through you. Or he's laughing but you know he doesn't mean it.'

She covers her face with her hands.

'Which one was he?' I say.

'Heinrich,' she whispers.

'Oh,' I say softly.

'Heinrich' had an encyclopaedic knowledge of every known fetish and was the inventor of some stuff I hadn't even heard of. There was a court case because of his contribution to one painting, a very detailed shopping list of oral sex preferences which didn't go down too well in Butte, Montana.

'Perhaps you owe him some royalties then,' I say but I can see what is worrying her. If he's crazy enough to molest his daughter on the net then he could have done Nails. Papa has been killing people since about 1940 although the ritual trimmings of this particular slaying still make it unlikely. For all I know. I don't want to discuss it while Sasha looks like this. She's subdued now, but it might easily go the other way. We might soon need to use one of her straitjackets for their original purpose, the restraint of the clinically insane.

'He's gone now,' I say gently. 'You don't have to speak to him again.'

'But he's my father,' she says, triple pianissimo.

'So what? It's only cyberincest.'

'It's not funny. And it's not just him. She thinks she's normal, but she's worse. I was raised on the land, part of a Christian survivalist sect. Raised "with love and the rod." '

There is nothing to do except wait for her to tell it.

'She was obsessed with naturism. Even when I was sixteen she made me do exercises in the nude. With her. Every morning. While the rest of the family had breakfast. In the same room.'

Torn between sympathy and the first signs of what pulp pornographers call 'mounting excitement', I decide it is best to maintain my father-confessor routine and hope the story keeps up to this promising start.

'Then we all had to take cold showers,' she says. Her usual self-confidence has now vanished and I wish I could help her, but the only way of doing that is to listen as the dread tale unfolds.

'Hm-mm,' I say, as neutral, and about as useful, as an expensive therapist.

'She would come in and check that we were really under the cold tap. Ten minutes each. Our bodies had to be cold all over. She would always check. Then we would always go on nudist holidays every summer. You have no idea what it's like always having to strip off every day.'

This from a woman who has shown the audience parts of her body that most people didn't even know existed. But the tone of her voice is cutting right through me. Then something very strange happens. She insists that we lay on the couch together so that she can go to sleep in my arms. It's nice to feel wanted, but all the time that's happening I'm dying to get back to the computer where I can access the 'Heinrich' files, which I do as soon as she is definitely asleep.

As soon as I start to read I wonder whether I will ever sleep again. As well as oral sex 'Heinrich' was obsessed with dismemberment, cannibalism and a fistful of other isms that I remembered Sasha used to love reading about. As long as it was safely on the other side of a computer screen.

In fact some of it was her fault. She was always asking him to elaborate on 'his darkest fantasies. Take me to your secret places.'

His half of these cyber texts were badly spelled, repetitive and whenever he got excited only capital letters would do. And he always used capitals for his favourite parts of Sasha's body. He seemed to like knives too. There was a lot of stuff about plunging a blade 'YOU KNOW WHERE'. It's much creepier if you've read one of Papa's erudite letters to his daughter, basically the same question Sasha's behaviour always poses: which bit is acting and which bit is real? And, like Sasha, he's probably got a whole bunch of other masks to try on from time to time.

I should sleep now but knowing that 'Heinrich' is within stabbing distance I just don't feel like it. And I really should look in on Rob.

Sasha stirs as soon as I do, also rather concerned about the results of our little experiment. I can't say I'm looking forward to seeing Rob again, but it will be intriguing to see what insights he will be able to offer us after his journey into inner space. I unlock the door to the Chamber to find that JC is snoring away next to an empty whisky bottle and there is a deathly silence from inside the freezer. Sasha and I look at each other long enough to realise that we both think Rob is dead. I shake JC awake and ask him if he had thought to check on Rob the last few hours or so. He mumbles something about being tired while we try to ignore what we are both thinking.

'I suppose the quicker we find out how many bodies we have to dispose of the better,' I say.

Sasha frowns at this typical example of English negative thinking as she flips the catches on the freezer. The remains of Nails are still face-down, under which the remains of Rob Powers are still encased in his latex bodysuit and hood.

Personally I don't see why Rob should have an easy transition back to this vale of tears so I slip one of Sasha's collection of voodoo death masks on as she demonstrates surprising strength and agility by flipping Nails to one side and whipping the latex hood off Rob's head.

He's still alive, or at least something is. It's probably not Rob Powers any more. The trembling gibbering grey-faced wreck in the coffin is trying to tell us something but he's not getting very far with it for the moment. What he needs now is medical attention and then therapy, something to gradually ease him back into the land of the living.

'Boo!' I say, as loud as I can, leaping towards him, but he doesn't seem in a mood for horseplay. Sasha unzips the bodysuit and frees him from his wrist restraints. She did, of course, use copious amounts of Vaseline when putting them on, but it obviously wasn't enough for this particular dark night of the soul. The cuffs are crusted with dried blood and minced flesh. His wrists will be scarred for life by the looks of things but at least he has a life. Or something has. The artist formerly known as Rob Powers is presently what he used to pretend to be in interviews: an inarticulate braindead zombie.

'Recalled to life,' I say, but he doesn't look like he's in the mood for swapping quotations from Dickens. He looks like a half-melted waxwork. I even feel a twinge of sympathy, for it is obvious he has been somewhere none of us wants to go. Will he be able to tell us something of his journey through the gates of perception into the reality of heaven and hell? Right now he doesn't look like he will be able to wipe the dribble off his chin. Or the bits that were Nails off the rest of him.

'Brandy,' intones JC. Sasha scurries off to fetch our alcohol supplies while JC and I stand round gawping at the victim like rubberneckers at a road accident.

'I've got Bach Flower Remedies,' she says on her return. JC and I both look to see if she's serious but she is.

'We need one of your biggest and best cattle prods for this job,' I say. 'Not a little bottle of diluted flower essence.' She scurries off to find the brandy.

I notice JC's piggy little eyes flare at the thought of the havoc Sasha might wreak armed with this implement while he was powerless to resist, but we have work to do, specifically the raising of the dead. I take my mask off as it's probably not as frightening as a hooded night in a coffin with a ritually murdered corpse. On acid. Indeed, Sasha might have done herself out of a gig because she might have to work hard to top that one.

'I have stood with Jesus on the cross. I have been to hell,' whispers Rob. 'I have seen the beginning and end of the universe.'

I'm pretty sure he doesn't know who we are right now. Which may be a good thing. You never know, he might feel slightly miffed at the people who gave him this once-in-a-lifetime opportunity to confront the dark side of himself.

Sasha, bless her, is genuinely concerned. She is rubbing back life into his spindly old shanks, murmuring in his ear and calling for herbal tea, something that falls on deaf ears as neither JC nor I wishes to be seen accepting an order in front of the other.

'It was just a dream, honey,' says Sasha. 'You're back with us now. Drink this.'

He takes the bottle of brandy and throws it against the wall.

'Begone, foul whore. Painted strumpet!'

Oh dear. It's all turning very ugly. JC rescues the bottle before it discharges more of the precious lifeblood within on to our already less than pristine floor and takes a few medicinal glugs. I can almost sense its fiery passage down my own gullet and imagine it settling on my empty stomach setting my brain alight with a cleansing blast of pure stupidity. Not an option available to me any more, so I settle for watching JC widen his gut and depleting his own already-meagre ration of brain cells. Meanwhile Rob is still aflame with the holy spirit.

He points a trembling finger at me and fixes his hollow eyes directly on mine. I feel the minutest twinge of guilt at the state of him, but he'll get over it. In time. Probably.

'Don't tell me,' I say. 'Let me guess. You were raised Catholic.'

'You will rot in hell. Your flesh will burn!'

He puts a lot into the last bit, so much so that he breaks down again and starts to weep.

'There, there,' says Sasha and gives us both barrels of her goddess Kali look before she reverts to Mother Teresa ministering to the sick.

'Before Monday at three! The ungodly will be punished!'

There is a short significant silence, during which Sasha, JC and I come to the same conclusion. Rob don't live here any more.

The next bit comes with a generous helping of spittle, delivered con brio and with a good deal of gesticulation.

'I have sat at the right hand of God! He has given me a mission! I must do His will!'

'Hood him and put him back in the box?' I say.

'And some fell on stony ground,' says Sasha to signify that this is time to shut the fuck up.

I drag JC into the kitchen, where I assemble freshly ground Amaretto flavour beans, cinnamon sticks and dinky little black cups and saucers. With sinking heart I put the question to JC. 'How would you like your coffee?'

'I'll have an American cup of coffee. With cream, two sugars. Or do I have to drink faggot's coffee as well as surrender my asshole cherry?' he says, puffing out his chest and rubbing a set of scarred knuckles with his other puffed-up, sausage-fingered hand.

'Well, don't look at me,' I say. 'I don't want your cherry and I doubt whether even Haskins would.'

His whole body relaxes at these glad tidings. Crossing the abyss in the Crowleyan sense is one thing, but some eternal verities cannot be tampered with.

'But Sasha might feel you would benefit from some internal exploration,' I say.

Although most of his facial flab remains motionless, he can't really suppress a surge of glee at this news.

'Have you seen "Big John" or "Thor's Hammer"?' I say. 'You could probably keep your average female elephant happy with one of those. What's the problem? It's good for your prostate.'

'You're English, right? What else should I expect?' he says, accepting the coffee with as much bad grace as he can muster. He sips it warily, as if I have somehow mixed in female hormones while his back was turned. Not that he plans to turn his back evermore on any male member of our little coven.

'You want to play by Uncle Aleister's rules, you have to acknowledge the bisexual nature of the human animal. Or at least confront what you are most afraid of.'

It crosses my mind that we should shut JC in a coffin with

some soap and water and see if he survives that, but we already have one basket case on our hands.

'Sounds like a pain in the ass to me,' he says with a rogueish smile to let me in on the jest.

'Don't worry, JC. You don't have to go through with it if you don't want to. With us, the customer is always right.'

'Maybe I don't want to be a sorcerer if it means wearing a dress, putting on make-up and listening to English faggot bands,' he says, toasting me with his coffee cup as he does so. 'You got a Danish?' he says.

'Something sweet and sugary? Like girls like?' I say and watch his eyes harden and one side of his mouth curl downwards in a surprisingly childlike expression of petulance.

'Whatcha' going do with Nails?' says JC.

The body. We must get the body out of the house today.

'Funny you should say that. That's the next step in your initiation.'

I explain to JC that any initiate must undergo a test of strength and his will be as simple as disposing of our corpse.

'And what will you be doing during this?' he says.

'Giving you directions. Come on. I'll tell you on the way.'

Back in the Chamber Sasha is rubbing Rob's shoulders as he stares hollow-eyed into space.

'Don't open . . .'

JC just has to open the freezer for a last look. I shut it right away but by then I have yet another death-mask image to remember Nails by. And more of that unique waft of his.

At four a.m. we excite no attention getting the freezer out of the house and into JC's big gleaming wagon, which has a video, fridge and neatly stacked piles of porn mags. His choices are predictably unimaginative: *Playboy, Penthouse, Big Ones*. There are also dog-eared copies of *Soldier of Fortune*. It's hard to know which ones will have been used more often for masturbatory purposes.

'Nice van,' I say. JC leaves me a space to expound on this theme, but I can't. His face registers contempt then he moves into a tried and tested routine.

'There's only one rule. We don't leave cans to roll around inside the mothership,' he says, glowering hard at the memory of someone who had recently transgressed the code.

'Right,' I say.

'Skin up, then,' says JC as soon as we are seated. He tosses me a five-pound pack of smoking tackle mounted on a mahogany block on which some asshole has carved a goat's head inside an upside-down pentacle.

'I can't take any more dope right now,' I say, at which he snickers cruelly and shakes his head.

'Well, I can,' says JC, puffing out his chest. 'Hell, yes.'

He switches the ignition on, triggering a sample of the *Star Trek* theme tune, but I'm past caring. Once under way the last two sleepless nights finally inspire me to stretch out on one of the bunks. I don't need the earplugs or the blind, just the darkness outside and the old *Star Trek* episode on the video.

When I awake Captain Kirk has landed somewhere inhospitable, and we have landed somewhere near the desolate meatpacking district on the waterfront. It's still dark enough to slide the cargo into the cold grey waters off the Bronx witnessed only by mutant seagulls and stray dogs with razorblade teeth.

As the ripples spread outwards over the choppy water, I wonder whether Rob will betray us now he is not very well and whether it might not be quicker just to climb inside with Nails. We heft the freezer into the water and watch it sink, neither of us coming up with anything to mark the passing of a human life.

'I wouldn't fancy a dip in that,' I say eventually, looking at the freezing, scummy water that probably contains more noxious chemicals than even JC's favourite American beer.

'I never learned how to swim,' says JC.

Really? He hears something as I rush at him, but by the time he is shaping up to do anything about it I have shoved him in the back and the Black Church of Eternal Hellfire has one less member. Or it will have in a minute as soon as JC has stopped coughing and spluttering.

Will his fat enable him to float? I watch for a while as he does more exercise than he ever managed in his entire life. My heart feels about as cold as the water that is inexorably claiming him even though his futile arm-waving is briefly impressive. Fuck you, JC, I think as his ginger beard disappears for the last time. Well, he was the only witness, and there was no way he was ever going to keep a secret. And this has absolutely nothing to do with the way Sasha sided with him against me over the little prank we played on Rob. Nothing at all. The waters have closed over JC now, a final baptism as he goes off to play air guitar in Valhalla.

So that's what it feels like. Murder while not under the influence of alcohol and dangerous drugs. It went by far too fast last time. You could get to like it, I think as I get into JC's wagon and roll back towards Manhattan.

5
Easter Sunday Evening

'YOU KNOW THE dictionary definition of fetish?' She's wagging her finger at me again, but I'm going to let it pass. ' "An object superstitiously invested with divine, demonic or erotic power, and as such held in awe and usually worshipped." '

'Punch line?'

'Well, look at Pazazu. He's all three together. We have to ask him.'

If I don't sleep soon there will be another fatality, one I might actually regret. I had thought my glamorous assistant would be pleased that JC is presently sleeping it off on the bed of the Hudson. Far from it. It only seems to have reinforced her theory that I might have done Nails. Despite her best efforts at spoiling my day, the righteous rush of triumph that resulted from snuffing him out is only just starting to pall now it's dark again. But I need hot milk and a warm bed right now. The last thing I need is more dubious magical ceremonies.

'Ask him?' I say. 'You don't mean . . .'

It had to come. Sex magick with statues.

'Steady on, old girl,' I say, in homage to those old British movies she devours with such relish. She never quite got over the disappointment of finding out that I'm not Hugh Grant. But then I keep expecting that New Yorkers will be interested in Miles Davis rather than Princess Diana or Benny Hill. It works both ways.

'Some say he was the consort of Lilith,' she says.

Lilith, female evil incarnate. Until the real thing arrived on the Grayhound bus from Michigan, standing five foot two if she ever wore flat shoes, which she doesn't, and possessing the most bewitching, entrancing pair of grey-green eyes this world has ever known.

'I'm better looking,' I say.

'Only just. You wanna watch?'

'What's the usual answer?' There's a sly twitch at one corner of her mouth.

'At least you don't have to lube up for this guy. He's so drop-dead handsome. Look, I've never been jealous of your female lovers . . .' I say.

'Because you jack off thinking about it . . .'

'But if you think I'm going to watch you get next to a two-thousand-year-old-gargoyle . . .'

'You're jealous!'

'At least I'm alive.'

'Only just. So he got a bad press, so what? You shouldn't still be hung up on childish anthropomorphic representations of good and evil anyway.'

Her tone is scathing, but I don't mind. I like having a front-row seat for Sasha's performances.

'Maybe he won't fancy you,' I say.

'He's a man, isn't he?'

'Get on with it,' I say, but by then she's into a slow limbo that is indeed making me feel jealous. What has he done to deserve this?

' "Sasha sashays on to the stage,"' she says acidly, quoting a critic who was unwise enough to let his hormones loose in an adulatory review. When she has gyrated around the demon a few times she gently lays Pazazu on his back and straddles him.

'How's he going to fuck you if he has no dick?' I say.

Sasha closes her eyes and starts to seethe. When she has wound down to some histrionic tutting she has this to say. 'Typical male. It's all penetration, isn't it? Paz and I are going to bond first.'

'Well, don't let me stop you,' I say and find a walkman to record whatever she says when she hits her trance, still half-expecting her to confess to the slaying. She starts to gyrate slowly over where the demon's dick would be.

'At least we won't end up with the spawn of the devil,' I say.

'I might be carrying your child, remember?' she says, and I blush to think that I had forgotten about our new hobby, trying to spread our particular virus. You may not agree, but we think there should be more of this me and Sasha stuff in the mix.

'You're afraid this is going to work,' she taunts.

'Afraid that you are going to really invoke something for a change instead of just blaming your mood swings and bad temper on some bogus demon.'

'You bastard!' A bust of Baphomet comes winging my way propelled not by telekinesis but by Sasha, who has lost control, if Sasha she be, right now.

'Who was throwing that?' I say. 'Lilith or The Scarlet Woman or . . .'

'I hate you!'

'Yeah, yeah, just climb back on him and tell us who snuffed Nails. Then we can all get some sleep.'

She actually responds to something I say for once, and soon

we are off again, waiting for a call on the psychic telephone. There might be twenty minutes of hyperventilation and chanting before she strikes gold normally, but she has obviously been affected by recent events. After only five minutes of ecstatic writhing we have a message.

'Yes! Aargh! Oww! Yes! Yes!' Her eyes pop open and her tongue lolls out of her mouth briefly. Is it her homage to *When Harry Met Sally?* No, it's the astral jury back from their deliberations. Her eyes burn with the fury of the possessed as she points straight at me.

'It's you! It's you! It's you! You killed Nails!' she says.

I keep waiting for her to collapse into giggles, but she seems to have truly lost it this time. She calms down eventually and claims ignorance of what she has just said. I will never know whether she is putting me on, so I go and make another coffee. I catch myself thinking that she might have tuned into my fantasies about killing Nails that morning, but then the triple espresso motivates me to spend another hour hurling accusations at our close friends and acquaintances, although we are still no nearer to discovering who might have gained access to our lovely home to perpetrate this unspeakable act. Every now and again I catch Sasha in the act of staring intently at me.

'I know what you're thinking,' I say. ' "He's killed before. What's to stop him doing it again?" '

Sasha is even evaluating this remark. How genuine is my annoyance? Is it all an elaborate sham? Just as I am about to start smashing things, right on the cusp of me picking up Pazazu and hurling him through the nearest window she holds a hand up like a traffic cop, one side of her mouth turned slightly upwards in recognition of her victory.

'We'll ask the cards,' she says a little later. 'Then you'll stop going on and on about it,' she says, a strange way to describe the masterful flow of eloquence with which I just summarised the main suspects. These are, in my view, the self-styled Satanic Adept who has the hump because of my infringement of copyright, anyone who might have known Nails was here and fancied a spot of ritual murder, and Christian and Gabriel, our cleaning slaves. As they are unbelievably puny and refuse to kill even cockroaches, it seems unlikely that they would do such a thing.

Apart from the man upstairs who is probably mad enough to have done it, like everyone else on the Lower East Side, the finger of suspicion would seem to be pointing at a certain pint-sized dominatrix who could easily have manoeuvred Nails into a position where he wouldn't have realised she was going to cut off his pride and joy.

I haven't confided my suspicions to her just yet but she knows somehow. It's one of the reasons she is glaring at me from time to time, although there are now nearly five years of other accumulated reasons why this might be happening.

'We'll use my special deck,' she says. Which means it's serious.

Too many punters know about the Tarot by now, and I wouldn't be surprised if even the Church of England had incorporated the cards in a desperate attempt to fill a few more pews. But this particular pack is different. Sasha has drawn her own Major Arcana cards, in black ink and red menstrual blood. All are concerned in some way with the practice of sex magick; most have some sado-magical resonance. To the initiate they all sing.

The devil is the Dark Goddess in Sasha's pack; she has painted the two of us as chained slaves ready to do her bidding. Some regard the card as a reminder to overcome the baser, fleshier sides of our natures, but however you interpret it it's nothing to do with the joke figure the Xtians made up to slander Pan, a perfectly respectable nature-god.

If that pitiful eunuch St Paul hadn't been so terrified of women we could all be running round the woods naked on a Saturday night, quaffing mead from horns and swallowing mushrooms by the handful with the government's blessing. Instead of which we have the pitiful spectacle of rational politicians pretending to be Xtians just to get elected. I digress.

Sasha has changed into a purple diaphanous robe and is flitting about lighting incense, ringing a small bell and humming to herself while waving her ritual dagger about.

'Can we start?' I say, losing my rag at the thought of a full banishing ceremony before we can get down to it. What with one thing and another I no longer care if we attract the wrong sort of demons. 'There is no audience,' I remind her. 'So you don't have to do your act.'

Sasha comes back to earth with a frown.

'We must be careful now we have Pazazu as a house guest,' she says. I invoke something rather less ethereal and more agricultural, at which she smiles fondly. 'My big grouchy bear,' she says.

It's a long time since she has used this endearment. I suppose I have proof that she loves me because she could easily dump me and move in with Rob, who would shower her with money and adulation. More important, he would make her the sole beneficiary of his will, which he has actually offered to do on more than one occasion. Without her I would have to sell bogus drugs to out-of-towners outside dance clubs and I would live . . . Give up. Don't know where I would live.

'You look like you've seen a ghost,' she says.

I shake my head to banish this pitiful vision. 'Just deal the cards, sweetheart,' I say.

She shuffles carefully then lays enough cards out to allow for almost any interpretation of anything.

'Well?' I say.

'Oh, no! This just can't happen,' she says, raising awe-struck eyes from the vision of doom on the tabletop.

I watch very carefully just in case she is rehearsing for some future performance, always a strong possibility, but it does indeed appear that the cards have triggered something unpleasant in her subconscious. Something bad enough that her eyes brim with tears, but she stops on the threshold of giving in to it.

'What is it?' I say.

'It's Christian and Gabriel. They must be in danger,' she says.

Well, I don't like them; they don't like me. I won't miss them at all.

'You didn't ask who the killer was?' I say, feeling a little short-changed. She reshuffles and deals three cards on to the purple silk square – Death, Justice, the Hanged Man, all of which I posed for.

'It's my lucky day,' I say. However sceptical you are, it's unnerving. Especially as she shuffled them properly and . . . she's got me at it now.

'It's you,' she says. 'And you could so easily have done it.'

'Could not.'

'Could so. Even the order the cards came out. Death.' She places one of her purple claws on the Grim Reaper. 'That's Nails.'

'Really?'

'Then Justice. How we will be judged by the Lord of Karma.'

'That's a relief. I thought it was going to be a jury of twelve of my peers.'

She looks at me for a moment before saying: 'They won't find twelve like you anywhere.'

'I'll take that as a compliment. The Hanged Man must be the chair, right?'

'You know better than that. It means stasis, uncertainty. You may never know who did it.' Her voice shrinks to a whisper.

'You might have done it yourself and have wiped the memory already. You could never admit to yourself that you could do such a thing and so . . . you hit the erase button and live to spend the rest of your life wondering whether you did it.'

She is just so creative. A never-ending stream of ideas that are never less than dazzling. I know the derivation of this one, the false-memory circus of a few years ago in which people were encouraged to think that they could have forgotten years of sexual abuse. But that doesn't excuse it. On the other hand she has watched me kick someone to death. And loving every moment of it. So she says. I often wish I could recover that particular memory. As far as I know those states of drunkenness I used to call automatic pilot are not recoverable by hypnosis even if I were susceptible to it, which I'm not.

'You've taken a lot of drugs,' she says. 'You've been under a lot of stress . . .'

'I think I would remember mutilating a close friend.'

Those words hang in the air while we both try to rummage through the half-digested Freudian junk we have retained from old magazine articles.

'You never called him that before,' she says, her accusatory index finger reminding me briefly of the bone the juju man points at a member of the tribe who is marked for death.

'Yes, Herr Doktor. I couldn't sublimate my love for him any longer, and the passion had to be expressed through extreme violence.'

'That's a lousy German accent.'

'What does it matter? I shouldn't have to say this. I didn't do it!'

Then the joke's over and she is actually staring at me, trying to get me to confess. I get up and walk over to the fridge. If she's going to be like that it's Miller time or indeed any other substance which will quell anxiety or stupefy the senses. But I can't drink, and as the only drugs available are hallucinogenics I am stuck with listening to Sasha accusing me of a ritual murder.

'You could easily have done it,' she says. 'You had means, motive and opportunity.'

What on earth has she been reading lately? Has she been at her stack of mouldy old green Penguins again? Purely so she can deconstruct them, of course, certainly not because she might be excited by some spinster detective unmasking a murderer in some cosy English village that never existed.

'I was in a deli eating pastrami on rye,' I say, just to shock her. I'm not supposed to eat meat or she'll leave me. She doesn't know, has never even suspected that I am constantly sneaking out for something clandestine and carnivorous.

'You bastard!' she says, eyes blazing and synapses fizzing with righteous indignation. In her world it would have been better to have eaten Nails than to have the occasional salt-beef sandwich. 'I'm sick of the sight of you!' she says, definitely not acting now.

'Don't worry!' And with that I employ the deadliest weapon at my disposal. I flounce off out of the house in a huff.

It takes about three blocks before I stop talking to myself.

How could she think I did it? Just because of a strategic decision to dispense with JC. And an unfortunate incident in Lewisham several years ago. It's ironic that despite the veneration Sasha usually shows for that most sought-after of dinner guests – the serial killer – I probably still wouldn't be allowed to play my Bartók CDs at home even now that she thinks I killed three different people. There's just no pleasing some people.

Sidestepping the bogus Ecstasy dealers round St Marks Place I am soon trying to switch my brain off in the company of other solitary misfits. Whenever domestic bliss palls, I always prowl around the late-night bookstores which right now are full of Princess Di books and attempts to out-gross *American Psycho*. And if I wanted that I could have stayed at home. What I need is a self-help manual. Something like *Women Who Kill and the Men Who Love Them*. Perhaps. Or in the light of yesterday's débâcle, *Teach Yourself Necromancy*.

The other bookstore patrons are as shabby as you would expect for New York literati, perhaps in defiance of the sun-gods of LA whom they look down on. Two dark intense guys in thrift-store clothes are conferring over a handful of texts by the door. 'Kathy Acker, *Hannibal Lecter Was My Father*,' reads one aesthete delightedly.

His friend essays the shortest nod of approval I have ever seen, barely discernible. He must be another writer.

'Great title, why print the rest of it?' he says sourly.

But there is nothing here that will counteract the rage inside me. I need noise and the quickest way to get it is to walk a few blocks to the Knitting Factory. This stuff used to be called Avant-Garde Jazz. Now you can call it what you like and no one has ever cared less anyway. It still sounds like cats on crack fighting in a wet pillowcase. I pick up my souvenir ear-plugs at the door, which prove to be a wise precaution.

The first band plays a number called *You are standing on my toe! You bastard! And let go of my nuts*! Least, that's the way it sounds. Yet somewhere else in this city, quite close at hand, young people with few clothes on and tight, taut bodies are jiggling about to repetitive trance music. I, however, am sitting on a rickety chair watching a Japanese male mime artist wearing only a condom. He is striking poses which enable me to satisfy myself on the subject of his anal hygiene while a lesbian cellist, amplified past the point allowed by the Geneva Convention, saws away as if she has a personal grudge against the audience.

I've been involved in show business for a long time now, but I've never seen anything like this. Probably for a good reason. There is a trumpet-player who isn't. As to the rest of the ensemble, I will only say that the soprano saxophonist has not put in the requisite millennia required to play the instrument in tune, but then who has? Someone else proves that the goddess does have a sense of humour by trying to coax rational thought out of the tuba.

The audience is full only of people like me who are hoping to foist their own efforts on the public in the near future, although full is a dangerous word to use in this context. There are probably more people congregating at the traffic lights outside asking for change.

If Sasha is seeking release she is probably memorising *Withnail and I*, frame by frame. It's a wise decision. Why anyone would want to cast themselves on the cold, unforgiving waters of live performance is beyond me. I know all this and I still go out of the house. Perhaps my presence here is a sort of flesh-mortifying attempt at redemption.

Which isn't working. Nails is still dead. We don't know who did it. Which only matters because it might have been Sasha. And I might end up picking up the tab for whoever did do it. They might come back. And Sasha and I might never trust each other ever again. The music howls on. It's still not as loud as what's happening inside my head. While I'm deciding whether sitting in the electric chair would be any worse than listening to this, there is a tap on my shoulder and I turn round to be confronted by a huge spam-faced carcass with mirror shades perched in his blow-dried blond hair.

He is wearing a very large distressed black leather jacket, perhaps hoping to borrow some of the rock'n'roll credibility of urban outlaws like Rob or maybe as a nod to American motorcycle cops or airmen, but the effect, as always, is to remind you of those American men who like to seek out strangers and thrust their arms up their fundaments.

A thick gold chain around his neck nearly hides a faded tattoo which says 'Cut Here'. By the look of his thick jowls his physique has a top layer of flab underneath which are great slabs of muscle, most of it honed at the taxpayer's expense as he has undoubtedly spent more time inside than out. You need steroids to look like that, which may have been where he lost his mind.

'Hello, mate,' he says, the Cockney accent and the inappropriate grin setting alarm bells jangling. I stare at the vulgarian for a while wondering whether it's safe to say 'Do I know you?' when I realise I have seen his picture in the tabloids many a time.

It's Jason Skinner, who may wish to discuss the death of his brother. There has to be some rational explanation for his presence.

I haven't asked Jason what he thinks he is doing in New York when he should be in Spain with all his mates. I haven't even said that this isn't fair, although it isn't. Ever since he touched some pressure point in my neck that made me melt off my stool at the Knitting Factory I have let him do the talking, although he prefers to grin inanely instead of sharing his feelings with me. Apparently the Knitting Factory was part of his New York Rob Powers Heritage Tour, as Rob has been known to hang out there. Which is typical of my luck. If there actually is reincarnation I will probably be coming back as myself.

The warm night air is a cocktail of Chinese spices, humid filth and Jason's aftershave. He is wearing so much that I can just about get a buzz from the alcohol in it if I breathe in hard.

We pass some big steel containers in a garbage-strewn alleyway.

I wonder whether I will be dumped in there before being tossed in the Hudson, from there to sail out to sea, perhaps one day the tide pulling my weary bones and funny English teeth back to my native land.

'Small world, eh?' he says. 'You haven't changed, though,' says Jason, big grin still in place. 'I got a photo of you from one of those dozy whores Sasha used to hang round with. I heard you were in New York, but I never ever would have thought . . .'

He jiggles a big bunch of keys in one of his massive heavily inked fists. 'Mate of mine called Jerry lets me use his flat. Got a gym in the basement. You can watch me work out. Then I'll work out on you. You look as if you could use some time in the gym.'

More rat-tat-tat laughter.

We enter a neurotically clean, normal person's flat. Holiday mementoes, framed pictures of Mum and Dad. Motor-racing memorabilia, mainstream erotica in a neat pile next to the couch. A wall unit houses rows of video tapes, all with the same white labels and computer-printed titles. There are three books, two of which are about the SAS.

'Let's not fanny about, eh?' he says. 'Let's get it over with.'

The gym is down some stairs in the cellar, and as he cuffs me to the wallbars at my wrists and ankles it occurs to me that this is what many s/m game players yearn for and can't get, a genuinely life-threatening situation. I'd still rather be playing mini-golf, all things considered.

Once he has stripped down to his shorts I can see the tattoos. His legs are almost black, covered in a massive Maori pattern of black intertwining slabs. Above the waist he is all technicolour, except for the faces of the Kray brothers rendered in black and white. I can't tell if he's one of those fitness fanatics who never like to miss a training session or whether he's trying to intimidate me, in which case he needn't have bothered.

I try not to think about how Sasha is going to cope with this. There will inevitably be guilt as she blames herself for the argument, but then she seems very resilient when it comes to coping with dead lovers. She's always wearing black anyway, so it won't be too hard to cope with my absence. And soon Rob will no doubt offer to step in. Take care of a few bills at first. Maybe pay her rent. Then move her into his place.

'I'm not ashamed to admit it,' says Jason. 'I cried when my brother died. When you killed him, that is. I used to love my little brother. I have to avenge his memory. But I thought his killer was going to be some hard man.' He casts an eye over my quaking frame. He produces what could be a thirty-eight for all I know or care, spins the barrel, then holds it against my forehead. I have a long time to whimper uncontrollably before he pulls the trigger.

'Look at you. You've even wet yourself,' he says, after the hammer clicks on an empty chamber. I was hoping he wasn't going to bring that up, but all in all he seems a rather crude fellow.

'You struck lucky that time,' he says. 'Wanna play again?'

'Look. It was an accident. I was drunk. I didn't know what I was doing.'

We both notice my hands are trembling.

'Ever thought of joining the SAS, mate?' he says. 'You'd be just right. Utterly fearless. Never say die.'

The laugh ignites briefly then dies down into a set of guttural grunts that go on long after he could possibly enjoy it. Each one of these is like a jab in my stomach.

'Now I know it's only you, I suppose I could walk away, but you are going to tell someone.'

'I won't,' I say in a quavering bleat rather than the reassuring baritone I had planned, which prompts more mechanical laughter that jangles every single nerve in my body before it has finished.

'You say that now . . .' he says, and he is probably right. It's bad PR for him to let me live.

'I heard you like Rob Powers. He's a friend of ours,' I say. My voice is ingratiating, whiny and utterly contemptible, but all of a sudden it doesn't matter. He's hooked.

'You know Rob Powers?'

'Intimately,' I say. 'In fact, I know things about him you are just not going to believe.'

He gives me one of his dead hard looks but there is not much I don't know about Rob Powers and I manage to return it.

'You sound like a fan,' I say.

' "Dancing on Delancey",' he says, very close to the way the great man himself does it.

'I'm on that! Playing the piano! You collect Rob Powers records?' I say. 'I've got rehearsal tapes. I've got songs that were never released. I've got tapes of gigs.'

'I've got a song for him. He's gonna love it.'

I suppose it's being hyper-fit that gives him the insane confidence to say that. Even my face isn't enough to put a dent in that grin. He just knows Rob is going to sing one of his songs one day.

'If he does like it he'll hate you for it, and if he doesn't like it you'll hate him,' I say. 'And in any case it's not that easy. People are always giving him songs. Why would he ever want to hear any? It just reminds him he can't write any more.'

'I'll put it on for you,' he says, bustling over with a walkman and headphones for me.

Before I can stop myself I realise I have groaned out loud. Jason looks like he's about to play Russian roulette again. 'Sorry. I've heard a lot of demo tapes in my time. Let me hear it.'

I used to dream of this – a producer literally tied down and forced to listen to tapes of mine. It seems that Sasha's theories on visualisation have once more proved accurate, except that some of the fine details need adjusting, as usual. The song starts off as a leaden minor dirge with ham-fisted acoustic guitar to the fore. Soon there is a preposterous croaking Dylanesque vocal to share with us some insights that don't rhyme or have any apparent significance. We learn some New York street names. There is a woman called Stella who may be the one for the song's narrator.

It all has the unmistakable stamp of the master, but I can tell Jason is the author of this piece, and not just by the regular lapses into his native Cockney. Although he is trying to remain poker-faced, he is actually shifting his massive bulk from one foot to another and even examining his fingernails. I keep nodding my head to the beat and smiling at him, but he can't even bear to look at me.

Even though his audience is literally helpless to escape, Jason looks as if he would be more at home up on a charge of murder at the Old Bailey than waiting for my verdict. As soon as the song finishes I say a lot of stuff I don't want to remember, ever.

'He's going to love it,' I say in conclusion.

'Do you really think so?' he enthuses. 'When can I meet him?'

'He was round at our place this afternoon. If you unlock the cuffs I can take you there.'

'Well. Sorry about that, but he was my brother.' He starts to unlock the cuffs. 'How come an English muso is such good friends with Rob Powers anyway?'

'Sasha, my partner, is his personal corrective therapist.'

'He's kinky? Rob Powers?' Jason unleashes a few gut-wrenching belly laughs that don't seem to affect his pale blue eyes very much. Eventually a mechanical hyena laugh winds down into sepulchral grunts of approval. Lavverly. 'Go on. Give us more of this stuff.'

'Celebrity anecdotes? OK. Have you heard of William Burroughs?'

He looks over and gives me a short contemptuous laugh.

'Well, I don't know what you've read in jail, do I?' I whine.

There is another gut-churning moment where I have to wait to find out whether I have taken a liberty or not.

'I'll let that pass,' he says. 'Course I have. Rob's favourite author. So I checked him out. *Naked Lunch*. Bollocks. Utter fucking bollocks. And the worst movie I ever saw.'

'Absolutely,' I say, shelving the Rob and Bill anecdotes.

'Who's this Sasha, then? Your "partner",' he says, letting me know what he thinks of people who talk like that.

'Sasha's his sex therapist. We have about fifty hours of him on video. Him and Sasha.'

I thought he would be pleased, but he's curled his lip in disgust.

'Never understood all that stuff,' he says. 'Well. I have got this thing about women's stockings.'

I wait, expecting him to say he likes being strangled with them or something, but he actually does mean that he likes women in stockings.

'We've all got our dark secrets,' I say.

'Don't take the piss now,' he says. 'You take me to meet Rob, then I'll decide what to do with you.' He laughs again then claps me on the back.

'I suppose I cared more about someone thinking they could kill my brother than about anything else. But you? You just don't matter. Funny thing is he was going to die anyway. Cancer spread all round his guts. You probably saved him a painful death. Have a drink.' He throws a pair of fresh jeans at me and while I'm changing produces a silver flask on which is engraved the legend, 'Stay Sober? Fuck Off!'

'I don't drink.'

'Don't be a *cunt*.'

I hold the flask in a trembling hand and raise it to my lips. Even breathing in the fumes of whisky brings back a lot of very bad memories. But how can anything can get worse than it already is?

I sit with the flask rested on my lower lip, letting the soft, smoky Lagavulin drift into my nostrils, very occasionally tilting it upwards by a millimetre or so to admit a droplet on to my palate as we sit joshing each other about our little misunderstanding.

Not really.

It's high-octane bourbon in the flask, and what with one thing and another I quite fancy a drink.

'That's it, mate!' says Jason, after I've emptied it. He brings over two bottles of Rebel Yell and throws the tops away.

'That's fighting talk,' I say, or rather gasp, as the room gently undulates and my head expands outwards and upwards.

'It's fighting whisky,' he says, approvingly. 'Have another.'

I slosh this one round the glass first and then let some of it evaporate in my mouth before swallowing. My throat is coated with sweet, sticky loveliness, as is the pit of my stomach. My eardrums are being pounded on by a tympanist who has slipped out to the pub before the performance, having just found out that his wife has left him for the conductor. Catching sight of the frightening boggle-eyed chip-toothed maniac in the mirror, I dodge out of sight while offering my glass for a refill. It is only after two more of these that Jason says: 'Steady on.'

He pours himself a measure that Oliver Reed would have raised an eyebrow at, then spreads out some white powder on a mirror, after which I don't even mind satisfying Jason's insatiable thirst for Rob Powers anecdotes. He actually records the next hour with his camcorder as part of his official Rob Powers Heritage Tour. By the time he has responded to my critique of Jim Beam as being too aromatic by swigging an inch of aftershave straight from the bottle, it really is time to go out.

At this point Sasha and I might spend hours arguing over whether we should see some off-Broadway theatre or catch a feminist collage of used tampons, my own preferences having been discarded early on, but with Jason in charge life is so much simpler. He wants to go to a sports bar, we go to a sports bar.

It takes a while to stop him driving, but finally he settles for barging other people off the sidewalk on our way through the Village. Some of the local young men walk in a half-crouch as if bouncing up and down on a pogo stick. They sometimes sway from side to side while they are at it. It's a territorial thing meant to signify strength, virility and the willingness to engage in mortal combat at the slightest infringement of their complex code of etiquette. I have often wanted to venture a criticism of this ludicrous affectation, but I never had Jason's knack for summing things up in a nutshell.

'Look at these cunts,' he says, and I can't disagree. 'Got the runs, mate?' he says, stepping into the path of a very white scabby guy who is bouncing his way into a pizza parlour. He is undersized and painfully thin, but I'm sure he is very good at beating his women up. Jason does his pastiche of the walk and there is nothing for the runt to do except scowl.

It's big grin time all the way until Jason's insouciance dips alarmingly as soon as we get to Christopher Street and we become the object of the occasional predatory look. Some of the crew-cut men staring at us are wearing leather jackets similar to Jason's, and all of a sudden he is hard-eyed and tight-lipped. I'm not going to say anything about that at all. Not in this lifetime.

Once safely inside the nearest sports bar Jason relaxes now he can drink weak American beer and watch men in crash helmets running into each other repeatedly. It's an exquisite torture to have to sit there with a mad euphoric rush building while Jason explains his betting system, but at least the transfusion of alcohol has released feelings of great love and affection for Sasha. I have a good wallow in that while Jason rattles on. I have always been good at mournful longing and worshipping from afar; it's just the bits where you have to spend all that time together that aren't so easy.

Jason is also in love, the springtime phase.

'Look at that,' he says, nodding at the barmaid. 'Look. At. That.' He stretches out each word to the utmost just as our barmaid's *embonpoint* stretches the fabric of her T-shirt until it might conceivably give up the struggle and rend asunder, leaving Jason to grovel helplessly at her waist while her jiggling, jostling breasts fall all over his flushed red face. She has fair hair, pink skin, blue eyes and her manner is as servile as a freshly clubbed seal. The whole package does absolutely nothing for me, but Jason is practically slobbering. I recall a strikingly similar tabloid picture of his wife, who was 'standing by' her man the last time he was at the Old Bailey on some trivial peccadillo or other. It was called the Tooting Torso Case if I remember rightly.

'You're a happily married man,' I say, draining another glass. I stop rubbing my fingers in the bottom of the glass and licking them when the barmaid looks at me a little strangely.

'I'd be even more happily married if I could have some of that,' says Jason fondly. 'Shell looked like that once.'

Cherie? Shirley? Perhaps it's Sally and the drink is getting to him, but the only person who is going to be carried out of here is likely to be me. It is not often that an alcoholic will be able to tell his partner that he was forced to drink by a homicidal maniac and I intend to make the most of it.

'Do you miss the wife?' I say.

'Not since I went into training,' he says. 'I hit her every time now. Silly fucking cow.'

'Excuse me, sir,' says the barmaid, as his shoulders heave up and down as another gut-wrenching laugh rattles the glasses behind her. 'Could you moderate your language?'

For a tense moment it could go either way, but eventually he smiles broadly at her, which is still frightening, and says: 'Of course, love. It's high time we fucked off anyway. Come on, my son. Let's go and have a real drink.'

While he lurches off to the men's room I wonder if I have finally got over my youthful crush on clods like Jason. With a wince I recall the butt-dumb twenty-year-old I was, consumed with the injustice of professional armed robbers being 'fitted up' by the police, as they used to say.

'Now I've passed forty they can't fit up armed robbers fast enough for me. In fact, if you ask me the only solution is to round them all up . . .'

'Round who up?' Jason is saying, and I didn't even realise I was talking out loud, never a good sign. In the next bar we have to lean right into each other's ears to say anything. The second time I get a mouthful of his bushy white earhole hair I've had enough. Finally Jason finds a bar where he feels right at home. There are perhaps twenty men fighting as we arrive.

'What's all that about, mate?' he says to the nearest non-combatant.

'It's the Gaelic football,' he says in a strong Irish accent.

'Well, it's not like the Irish to quarrel,' I say, uncharacteristically courageous in the face of some dark glances in our direction, but then Jason is a big tough guy and I am very drunk. The fight is gloriously exhilarating to watch, but eventually it winds down to nothing except a very small man repeatedly attacking a much bigger one, who clubs him off. But he keeps on coming. The tall, slightly less stupid one flattens the little guy's nose and great gouts of claret spurt everywhere. Then the little man has another go. Slowly and carefully the tall one blacks his eye. Then, while it's still closing, the little guy is back and at him.

'He's game, isn't he?' says Jason, genuine admiration in his voice. 'Why doesn't he pack it in?'

'That's *Irish* fighting,' says a stooped old man proudly. Jason claps the guy on the shoulder, practically dislodging his false teeth in the process.

'Will you have a drink?' says Jason, not noticing the waves of hostility we are attracting.

'Well, now, I don't drink any more,' says the old man, eyes twinkling. 'But I don't drink any less, mind.'

He shows us his gums as he cackles away mechanically while we call for drinks from the hostile barman, who is obviously getting a grant from the Irish Tourist Board for his portrayal of a surly red-faced idiot. It's not often you see gumboils these days but another old man nearby has managed one, a great gleaming specimen out of which grows a single long white hair.

The Pogues come on the jukebox, setting off a rattle of glasses and a bobbing of heads. The natives are not particularly enamoured of Jason's Riverdance impression, which sends some empty stools flying and finishes up with the artiste himself flat on his back. Jason settles that one by buying a round of drinks for the bar before a long argument about the relative merits of Rob Powers over Shane McGowan develops. I'm ready to weep at the thought that these two imbeciles should be considered to be musicians at all, but the debate rages on around me until the living apparition of Shane McGowan's pus-ugly face appears on MTV.

'Turn it up,' jabbers someone nearby. Mr McGowan is endeavouring to talk in response to some probing question put to him by the interviewer, something like: 'Who are you?' He's having great difficulty framing the reply.

'He's a drunk, drug-addicted sack of shit,' Jason is saying, although it comes out 'Shack of schittt!'

'With funny teeth,' I say.

'Well, you can talk, Goofy,' says Jason, but before he can start in on me a guy taps him on the shoulder and chins him. It's a good punch, but as Jason rebounds from the bar he grabs a glass, smashes it and soon there is a scream from the man holding his face in place while thick red blood leaks through his fingers. Jason chortles gleefully then stamps on both of his feet and knees him in the nuts. He then takes a step back and kicks his descending chin hard. There is a clicking sound and a strangled groan that makes even my flesh creep, drunk as I am. Jason's lizard-skin loafers are now ruined, the guy on the floor is twitching in a way that is not pleasant to look at and we are suddenly facing an angry mob of drunken men who do manual labour all day and then pulverise their brains and livers all night.

Perhaps that's unfair. They may well put in a lot of gym time developing their massive shoulders and biceps while working as brain surgeons and arbitrageurs before going home for a dry sherry and a quick riffle through the *Cantos* of Ezra Pound, but my money's on the construction industry.

There is brief frozen moment in which to contemplate the difference between my love of violence, from a safe ringside seat, and this more hands-on approach.

As the wave of muttering micks breaks over us I have only

one strategy, which is to kick whoever is in front of me in the kneecap. When it works it's awesome, but this time I don't connect and the second punch has me on the canvas huddled in the foetal position.

It's then I remember the cock rings I have been wearing for so long I don't even notice them anymore. One kick in the nuts and we could be talking massively swollen gonads and amputation. I picture myself as Sasha's eunuch, pigtailed and perched on a cushion eating Turkish delight with a scimitar close at hand for unruly clients.

A boot in the ribs reminds me of the distance between my fantasy life and reality. In the course of the average day's bitter seething hatred I probably spend more time fantasising about violence than I do about sex, and even some of that sex is violence, according to spoilsports like priests, shrinks, doctors, the police and the general public. I'm usually the one deciding which ribs to break, but now the boot is on the other foot.

Before they can cripple me, the sound of a single gunshot reduces the bar to silence – that is, just the sound of drunken morons fiddling and piping away like the hounds of hell.

'Nobody move. Get up,' says Jason, with an admonishing toe in my ribs. I do my best. Once upright we manage to back out of the bar while they glower at us, one hothead almost ready to break ranks and rush us. The tension of the standoff is somewhat reduced by the two of us losing our footing as we take the stairs backwards, but Jason's grip on the gun never wavers.

'Well, they were a bit touchy,' says Jason as soon as we hit the street.

'What are we going to do?' I say, utterly frantic that we will be arrested. They don't even like litter in Greenwich Village, never mind gunfire. Jason smiles down at me, hails a cab and laughs as I cower on the back seat, hands shaking and teeth chattering.

'Well, I fancy a night in, after that,' I say hopefully, giving the guy directions for our place. Sasha's always saying we should have some people round. 'Would you really have used that thing?' I ask.

'It's a replica,' he says. 'It fires blanks. And we were acting in self-defence anyway. You don't know anything, do you?'

'Nothing useful,' I admit, but I still want to go home. And suck my thumb underneath a warm duvet. 'Do you want to see some Rob Powers stuff? I got videos, unreleased tracks, personal stuff.'

'Now you're talking. Got anything to drink?'

'Ever tried chilli vodka?'

6

Easter Monday

IT'S TEN A.M. AND JASON is still eagerly devouring photos, tapes, correspondence and all the other Robabilia I can put my hands on. We are still drinking, although the white powder has dematerialised. Now it's gone I am starting to be very concerned about Sasha's continuing absence until I find a note she wrote for me underneath a pile of Chinese takeaway cartons.

'Dear Matt, Rob asked me to go to the country with him. He needs looking after. Back Tuesday.'

I have three kisses on the bottom of the note but no freshly minted poetry about how great I am or drawings of little fluffy bunnies or Lilith astride her version of Beelzebub, who tends to be bald with the same tattoos I have. This withdrawal of privileges would normally be a stinging rebuke but, surfing on a great wave of Jim Beam as I am, I can't say I'm bothered until I remembered Rob mentioning three o' clock Monday as some sort of threat before. Quite recently, in fact. For once there is some point in having a Rob Powers completist on the premises.

'What does three o' clock Monday mean in Rob's world?' I say.

'You're joking! Don't you know that? Three o' clock Monday. It's in "Killing Time".'

I'm starting to sober up.

'What about it?'

'Keep your hair on, baldy. Monday, three o' clock, he kills his mother.'

And how many times does Sasha get to be mother in her therapeutic practice? The more I pace up and down the more it seems likely that this might be the day the worm turns.

'I'm worried about Sasha,' I say. 'She's at Rob's place in upstate New York. He had a bad trip the other night and I think he could be dangerous.'

'You could actually take me there?' he says, and there is a shining light in his eyes as he realises that the grail is within his grasp.

'Someone would have to drive,' I say gloomily, realising the impossibility of this.

'I'll drive. You stupid cunt. We'll have a quick espresso. This is the business. I'll get me camcorder.'

We walk through the Village in a cloud of sweat and whisky, invading an upmarket coffee bar where we cause a slight stir among the movers and shakers ordering their mid-morning jolt.

Jason's eyes are half-closed as he proffers a Chelsea FC souvenir thermos flask to the help.

'Don't faff about, mate. Fill her up,' says Jason, on his second attempt at climbing on to a stupidly tall and thin stool at the counter. It takes a while to establish that Jason does indeed want fifteen measures of espresso with whipped cream and sugar, and then people turn to watch us as we leave.

As we both collide trying to take the door at the same time someone says, 'It's Laurel and Hardy.'

Luckily Jason sees the funny side and we manage to get to his mate's underground garage without shedding blood, crunching bones or waving that gun of his around. I couldn't care less about Porsche 911s, so Jason gets the hump as I fail to admire his shiny blue fetish object. It seems a bit cramped to me, even without Jason's unfeasibly large body and big hair, but the stereo works all right, giving us the chance to check out more of Rob's monotone droning. Jason refuses to answer questions on his life of crime or anything else interesting and instead counters with detailed questions about Rob Powers. By the time we cross the George Washington Bridge I've decided to give myself up if we are stopped by the cops, but Jason is just warming up.

'In the studio. Does he plan in advance what's going to happen or does he just, like, make it up?'

After I have stopped groaning I decide not to tell him that Rob's one mode of composition is plagiarism. Usually whatever anyone says or plays anywhere near him will probably end up on the track. If the guy delivering the coffees knocks on the door three times, Rob will be seized by the brilliant inspiration that what he needs is percussion – say, three taps on a woodblock?

'Come on, you've done some work for him,' says Jason.

'Rob nicks what he can and hopes no one will notice. He's been at it for years. You think you're a thief? You've no idea, mate.'

'Nah, come on. You were on "Dancing on Delancey".'

More salt in my wounds. I remember Sasha arranging for me to play a session for Rob in exchange for post-production work on one of her film snippets. It's earned more money than anything else he's done recently. I have the glory. Rob has the money.

'What happens is that we do our best to try to match the

concept Rob already has inside his head,' I say, almost choking from bile. 'It's hard, but sometimes we come close.'

Jason nods sagely, after which I give up and tell him anything that will keep him driving to Rob's place. Neither of us feels comfortable once the urban landscape recedes, but Jason has a routine to mark the transition. Whenever we pass a solitary figure doing something agricultural in a big green space, Jason says: 'Now there's a man who is outstanding in his field.'

He laughs a lot the first time he says this and is practically cracking a rib by the tenth. It's meant to annoy me, and it does. But not as much as the ceaseless blather about Rob.

'Is he writing anything new?'

'Yeah. Cheques with Sasha's name on them,' I say. 'He said three o' clock Monday afternoon. How are we doing?'

'You worry too much,' he says. 'It's probably a lot of fuss over nothing.'

Eventually we reach a farmhouse well away from what passes for a main road around here, an isolated refuge ideal for ritual dismemberment. I curse JC once more for getting us into this mess. Rob had always been fairly docile before his night in the freezer with Nails's corpse, as irritating as any other passive-aggressive, but we knew where we were with him. Now he has discovered his inner child I hope Sasha has found a way to deal with it. We roll through the gate past the notice telling us not to trespass and then park by the farmhouse on some loose, noisy gravel.

We don't have long to wait for our host, who appears in his usual leather jacket and jeans but without the invisible 'Kick Me' placard he used to wear. I wonder whether we should try to patent our form of shock therapy – a rotting corpse, a latex hood, confinement and a tab of acid. Just wait until the behaviourists get hold of it. Rob's eyes are colder and harder than I've ever seen them. He is actually standing up for once rather than slumped diffidently. Jason, still not believing his luck, walks over to his hero and extends a beefy hand.

'You don't know me but . . .' he is saying.

I'm walking past Rob to see if Sasha is inside the house when Rob pulls some effete-looking weapon and shoots Jason in the chest. It's a girlie gun, not the full Clint Eastwood number, but it makes a loud bang and the blood spreading over Jason's stomach is real. He is still standing for the second one, which floors him. As he twitches on the floor there is a puzzled look on his face as Rob puts one through his head.

'He only wanted an autograph,' I say, when the echo has died down. Rob points the gun straight at me and I have to try to think of some last words, but I can't. It doesn't seem to matter if he shoots me or not.

'Does this mean the European tour's off, then?' I say finally.

He's still staring at me.

'Drag him inside,' he says. 'I've got plenty of bullets left.'

I heft Jason's bulk over the threshold and reflect that he didn't even get a hello from his hero. And he never got to play him his song.

'Is Sasha here?'

'She's downstairs. You first.'

Inside it looks just like places I've lived in on my own, as if it's been recently burgled. I follow his directions, glad to be alive although more than a tad apprehensive as to what may be waiting in the cellar. I am soon in the sort of working environment Sasha always lusted after, a big well-lit space full of racks, pinions, hoists, cages, rails full of rubber outfits and tables spread with paddles, crops, whips and some implements I don't even want to look at, never mind find out what they are used for.

The overpowering scent is of rubber, leather, sweat and used amyl nitrate. Which at least holds out the possibility that Rob might have a heart attack while he's killing us. And centre stage on a raised podium are two studded black leather crosses, one of which is occupied by Sasha. She is wearing a tight black latex bodysuit, her hair plastered down on her head with her own sweat. There are ropes at her ankles and wrists to keep her in place, but she has to stand upright on the small platform provided, otherwise she would be unable to breathe. Hope flickers briefly in her eyes as I appear but is quickly replaced by mute acceptance of whatever is coming next.

Perhaps, like me, she is thinking that we should have sought out some other line of work, but it's too late for regrets. It's a long time since we all went to Sunday school and there's no going back now.

'Take your clothes off, then get this on,' he says, tossing a similar latex suit at my feet. 'Do it or I'll shoot her now.'

Getting crucified is probably worse than getting shot, but I don't want to get him any more annoyed than he already is so it's easier to cooperate. The inside of the suit has been powdered so that it slips on easily. It would feel good normally, but a tight rubber sheath is not the sort of garment I would want to be found dead in. He doesn't give me a single chance all through the process of being taped then tied to the cross, and when it's done Rob dances around us snapping away with a Polaroid. As each one develops he examines it then tosses it at our feet. Sasha has to crane her head to examine the images, of course. Even in her death throes she just has to know what face she is presenting to the world. I suppose she is already hoping that these pictures will be found one day, that her last work of art will be preserved.

'I've dreamed of this for years,' says Rob, grinning unpleasantly. 'And all I had to do was lure Sasha here with a promise that she could re-create her famous Crucifix Art. And I was certainly as good as my word.'

'You know, I always thought this was unrealistic,' I say. 'Some megalomaniac hanging around to discuss why he is going to kill people and explaining the puzzling events that led up to the dreadful predicament the protagonists find themselves in.'

It's a bit of a mouthful for a man facing certain death, but the grandstand view from up here makes you a bit preachy. Comes with the territory.

'Wrong again,' says Rob with a snicker. 'What could be more enjoyable than watching you suffer? It's a drag that you won't beg. Yet. But you must know that asphyxiation is a terrible death. And to die knowing that you are responsible for your lover's death . . .'

'Well, I wouldn't know about that. "She made me do it" is going on my tombstone.' I still feel surprisingly calm. Maybe Rob isn't the only psycho round here.

He presses a button and the image of a green hill is projected behind us. From where he is sitting we are atop a hill in Galilee. It's all starting to look a bit final now.

'You know, I'll always love you, babe,' I tell Sasha.

'I love you,' she says. But then that impish look that indicates a sudden shift of identity comes in her eyes. 'Rob, there is something I always wanted to tell you,' she says in her deceptively sweet and innocent voice. That sound usually cues up a steel toecap in the shins or, even worse, one of her devastating sighs. You don't want to be on the wrong side of one of those, believe me.

'Oh, my,' he says, actually rubbing his hands together and gloating. It looks like bad acting but it's real life. He really has flipped. 'This is the bit I have been waiting for,' he says, eyes glinting, a little stream of spittle leaking from one side of his mouth.

'Give me the pitch,' he says, snickering as he does so. ' "Why I should be allowed to live", in twenty-five words or less. What are you going to offer me, Sasha, honey? Be my slave? Like you are the only whore offering those services. You are going to pay for betraying me.'

As much as a person facing certain death can be, Sasha is unmoved. 'You are not talking to your mommy now, Robbikins, you're talking to me,' she says firmly.

It's a brave try but he is still raging. 'You just wanted my money. You never cared about me.'

'Well, we all have our crosses to bear,' Sasha replies, looking over towards me, but I'm in no position to share a high five. Rob steps up to the cross and hits her as hard as she used to hit him.

While she's whimpering I'm vowing all sorts of vengeance which is cut short by Rob, who needs to share.

'You want to know why I'm not going to use the ball gags on you?'

Sasha has lost it for the moment so it's down to me to try to keep him on the planet earth.

'Why aren't you going to use the ball gags on us, Rob?' I say.

'Because I want to hear you beg. I want to have it on tape. With the rest of my collection. So I can enjoy it whenever I want.'

He opens a studded leather chest bound by what may be gold clasps and shows us two rows of neatly stacked video tapes with very small neat handwriting on the labels.

'Wanna know what happened to Christian and Gabriel?'

'Not particularly,' I say.

'You have to listen to me now,' he says, each word etched slowly on to a backwash of churning rage.

Well, that will make a change. At last, a chance to reverse the massive injustice of the last few decades of being showered with wealth and adulation.

'Check this out,' he says and then clicks on a tape of two hooded and bound figures in this very cellar. Rob is masked for this, but there's no mistaking those bandy legs or the three-pound weights hanging off his tackle. This is probably the one time Rob actually put any effort into his art, but I don't think congratulations are in order right now.

The scrawny figure on the cross thrashes about as Rob pours water through a funnel into the lining of the hood, which swells up gradually. A sideways glance at Rob confirms my suspicion that repetition is strengthening his bond with this tape. The more he watches it, the more he likes it. And when he's killed us we will enjoy a sort of immortality in this very cellar – endless reruns until the tape snaps or he finds another set of victims.

'Look! He really thinks he's drowning even though he knows he's still breathing,' says Rob, his voice shot through with a grisly fascination. For the first time in my life I feel sympathy for Christian. Even in the context of a consensual game, the water inflating the hood's inner lining must have been unbearable. And knowing that the person in charge of your destiny had every intention of killing you . . .

'Just imagine that!' says Rob, a somewhat manic gleam in his eye as he points at the screen. 'I've been through it. It really does feel like drowning.'

I remember Sasha telling me about that one. Maybe she even did it to Rob. Funny, that. Perhaps this is the karma of which the white witches always speak, although Sasha liked to say that that sort of sloppy thinking was just hippie bullshit that should have died out with loon pants. It's high time she magicked us off these crosses, of course, but she looks a bit drowsy: maybe that is what is dulling her awesome powers.

'I can't wait to hear you beg,' says Rob. Can't be long now, but it's not prudent to say so.

'I don't care what you do,' I say. 'I would rather die with Sasha then spend ten years waiting for her to fry. Or take the rap myself. Someone tried to frame us for Nails. At least this way is relatively quick.'

He thinks about that for a few seconds, as I hoped he would.

'You'd get off. She would pay for a good lawyer. The "abuse excuse".'

That sets him off cackling again. We really shouldn't have left him in that freezer so long. It hasn't done him any good at all.

'Have you considered therapy?' I say, but he's a tough audience. He only seems to like his own jokes. There's one thing still bothering me, though, and once that's cleared up we can get on with slowly suffocating to death in peace.

'You did Nails, right?' I say, croaking a bit as I dehydrate.

'Wrong,' he smirks. 'I know who did, though. But I'm not going to tell you.'

Well, that's showed us, but luckily Sasha has the appropriate strategy.

'You were on the radio. How could you know?' she says.

He can't resist appearing smarter than her for once.

'I rang in to cancel,' he says. 'They played an old interview tape. Remember the way you would never let me get in that necro freak DJ's coffin? And you know I've always been an Edgar Allan Poe fan!'

Life sure is a bitch, but I'm going to shut up for once while he tells it.

'I was inside the coffin when some old fat white-haired guy turned up pretending to be a plain-clothes detective. I could see through the airholes while he was slicing Nails to bits. As soon as he got into it he was raving away in German.'

Guess who? Sasha has closed her eyes to cope with this revelation.

It's yet another betrayal. Her chest heaves and she starts to sob. Time for wise words to console her, but 'Cheer up, it may never happen' doesn't seem appropriate.

As the afternoon wears on we drift in and out of consciousness, taking the occasional refuge in dreams and visions, but it always comes back to what is becoming hard to ignore. We are not going to get off these crosses.

If only we could leave this flesh, bone and gristle stuff behind and float off somewhere. It doesn't seem like a wise decision to carry on suffering purely for Rob's benefit. Sasha looks like she might have checked out already. So . . . this is it. The thing I never achieved while I was in my right mind: astral travel. Or death, in this case.

Just as I am getting used to looking down on my weary pain-wracked body from somewhere up near the ceiling my mouth fills up with some sour fluid that is bitter enough to wrench me back to the vale of tears. Pain floods through me as I crash back into my old self, not helped by this foul acrid taste in my mouth.

'What's this?' I croak. I can now see that Rob is holding a bath-sponge on a stick.

'Thought you might be thirsty,' he whines.

Biblical precedent is not good but I suck on the sponge anyway. I never did like balsamic vinegar.

'You do realise you're just perpetuating the stereotype that all s/m games-players are potential serial killers,' I say, but he's run out of some essential item.

'Don't go away,' says Rob, taking the stairs. 'I'll be back with something you're really going to enjoy.'

The overpowering odour is still rubber, although sweat is starting to manifest as we struggle to ease our agony. There is also a faint trace of the sandalwood oil with which the suits are lined, another one of Sasha's ideas. This is supposedly an aphrodisiac, if you weren't about to die. Although for many on her mailing list this would be the icing on the cake and the cream in their coffee.

'What do people get out of this?' I say to Sasha. 'I've always wanted to know.'

'It's an adrenalin high,' she says in a voice eerily drained of her usual manic intensity.

'It's exciting. I can't deny that,' I say. It would be even better with the vague hope of someone struggling against all the odds to rescue us. But we are irretrievably doomed. As we move about to try to minimise the pain we generate even more sweat to squelch around inside the latex suits. I suppose Sasha can die happy now she's finally shed her last few ounces of surplus fat.

'If only the mainstream press knew you could lose weight with bondage,' I tell her. 'Then it would be the religion for the next millennium. Fuck Xtianity. Trim your figure with latex. But what about the men?'

'Men aren't vain?' splutters Sasha. 'You're telling me men aren't vain? I bet that on the cross Jesus was thinking: "Well at least my ribs are sticking out and thank Christ this beard covers my double chin".'

'Thank Christ?'

She puts her tongue out and shakes her head at me. 'I'm dying,' she says. 'I can't concentrate.' Her voice is wistful, her smile tinged with the acceptance of defeat, something I would never have expected from her.

I regret to say that I'm back to my old tricks of projecting negativity into the future. With some justification, perhaps.

'I know. Why don't you convert him to Xtianity? Then he'll let us off.'

Sasha raises a weary snicker at that. 'You're sure? I had an abortion once. People have seen my naked body. That's enough for crucifixion for most Xtians.'

It's a generalisation, but she does get mail like that from Texas.

'Maybe we should convert,' says Sasha. 'We're not going to get off these crosses. Maybe we should enjoy the experience.'

'Always look on the bright side? I'm not so sure. But I'll say this for Jesus. What a franchise system! Makes McDonald's look like a corner shop. And when you consider the product doesn't even work . . . He's done very well for himself.'

'Hush your mouth,' says Sasha.

I forgot she's a recovering Catholic. They might say they have got over it but they never have. Not really.

'Maybe we will be saved by the Second Coming,' says Sasha.

'Yeah, right. I thought you were always late for everything. What about him?'

'God will not be mocked,' she says sleepily.

'Oh, won't he, now? Oi! Beardie!' I can still do a South London accent. Should come in handy. 'Wait till I get up there, mate. I'm going to 'ave you, you facking cant.'

Even a half-hearted snicker hurts. Good for morale, though.

Rob's not so happy now as he hears us joking in the face of adversity like some plucky little Cockneys in a film about the blitz, but he soon puts paid to all that. 'Nearly three o' clock,' he says. 'That's when I'm going to break your legs.' He picks up a baseball bat and twirls it in the air.

'It's too late,' I say. 'You should have done us on Good Friday.'

'I said three o' clock Monday and I meant it. I'm jealous. You will be on the right hand of God this very day.' With that he leaves us again.

Sasha tells me a lot of stuff I never knew about her childhood for a while, but I've run out of snappy rejoinders. I'm finding it hard to get the images of Sasha's Crucifix Art out of my head. Especially when Rob is giving us such a unique perspective on the contemporary relevance of religious iconography.

Sasha is hanging from her arms now rather than being supported by her feet. She can't have long to go.

'This is the best chance we will ever have to channel some of that Jesus stuff. So it's time to give us a miracle, you know, resurrection would come in handy,' I say, and her eyes light up. I only hope she's thought of something.

Rob bounces back in and picks up the bat, glancing at his watch. He grins at me for a while and I close my eyes while I look for loopholes. Then I remember the way Nails lives inside my head.

It seems to fit with something I read in one of Sasha's astral guidebooks.

'There's another type of reincarnation, Rob,' I say. 'Something taught to us by our master called the Black Rite. Which is more than just haunting you. When we die we are going to concentrate real hard. You might not notice at first but soon you are going to have Sasha and me as house guests.'

'We are both going to try to push you out of your shell,' says Sasha in a very calm, determined, rational voice that is much scarier than the cackling witch she is also very good at. Rob tries to smile but he can't.

'It's going to be a fight, of course. You won't give up easily,' she says. 'Remember the way it was a drag sharing an apartment? Just imagine the three of us in one head? There won't even be room anymore for Mommy, your biggest problem.'

'Shut up about her.' His face twists and darkens but Sasha still has him on the end of her leash. And if she jerks the choke chain suddenly and sharply he is always going to do her bidding.

'You will lose your mind gradually,' she says, slowly and steadily, just like those hypnotism tapes that never work on me. 'There may be times when you come back but we will cast you out. You will never be sure whether you hear my voice or Mathew's voice or your own. Finally Mathew and I will use your body for our purposes, and you will be cast adrift to wander the astral plane for ever. You will never be reunited with your mother. You will for ever dwell in the silence.'

A whimper escapes from between Rob's hands, now covering his face. His chest is shaking. I suppose it's the accumulated memory of hundreds of sessions in Sasha's Chamber or his childhood or the multiple addictions or fame then lack of it or his elder brother telling him he wasn't wanted or for all I know when he found out there was no Santa Claus, but something is wiping out every trace of the Rob Powers that was about to kill us. She starts to chant once more while Rob falls to his knees and lets his head loll on his chest, which is more the Rob we know and love.

'You cannot kill me,' says Sasha. 'I am woman. The eternal goddess. I will endure.'

He is still and silent, unable to do anything except stare at the floor. If I could move my arms I would applaud. Sasha has the old Satanic light beaming out of her eyes now.

'Remember when I had you fitted for your piercings?' she says to Rob.

We get a sullen nod in return.

'You already knew they weren't for your supposed pleasure,' she says, a certain singsong quality in her voice. 'But you thought they were for my enjoyment. Or it was merely a commercial transaction. Not so. The reason we took so long putting them in, the reason we waited so long for the appropriate astrological conditions was that each and every one of your piercings is a talisman. I concentrated long and hard on those bits of metal even before they went into you. That is why you struggle so hard to break the chains of your dependency on me. I am inside your very body. As well as inside your mind.'

She's hooked him. His eyes are like saucers and his mouth has dropped open. Her voice takes on a more taunting quality now.

'Mathew and I charged each and every one of those piercings. We had a lot of fun doing it too.'

Which is actually true, no doubt accounting for the conviction in her voice. I remember thinking what a waste of perfectly good blood and sperm at the time, but you never know when these things are going to come in handy.

'All the metal in your body has been soaked in our vital essences, Rob. That's why you can never win. The more pain we suffer, the stronger our magical abilities are. We are inside your body. We are inside your mind. We are you. Kill us and you kill yourself. Slowly. And painfully. You will call out for me. But I won't be there for you.'

That's got him. He snarls and starts to pull at his numerous nipple piercings. The rage grows until he rips one clean out, bellowing in pain as he does so. Which is fine, but he has twenty-three separate piercings including three simultaneous Prince Alberts. Some are easy to remove but most are not. He might not fancy ripping that little lot out. He might bleed to death in front of us. Which would enliven our last moments no end, but we would still be on these crosses. But there's no doubt about it: the balance of power is tilting our way. He rips a thick vertical dagger piercing out of his other nipple. Ouch. And there's a lot more to come.

'My magick is stronger than yours,' he says, but he is veering back towards submissive mode. 'I just hired your services. You never knew the real magick. What is on these tapes is the real work. One day the world will understand.'

He is nodding his head vigorously as his nipples weep fresh blood. His eyes are glittering as he unscrews another one carefully, but a lot of stuff will come out only with a wrench and I doubt if he is up to it. I saw a lot of that stuff go in, and just watching it made my eyes water. He is still staring defiantly at Sasha, but she has closed her eyes and started a chant that I recognise as one of her party pieces, an invocation of Lilith, the Dark Goddess. I used to be an agnostic in these matters but I concentrate hard, too, and join in the words where I can remember them.

Rob doesn't like it. 'You bitch! I'll silence you for ever.'

'You can't,' she says, and that drives him to rend more of his flesh asunder. He has probably already suffered enough to be canonised, but Sasha is proving hard to win over.

The chant continues. His crazed eyes find mine. 'Make her stop!' he shrieks.

Which just proves he lives alone these days. Make her stop? I can't make her get me a cup of coffee. I can't shrug my shoulders roped to this thing, so I just stare at him for a while as he occupies himself by ripping more steel out of his chest. When Rob takes a break from self-mutilation I notice he is back to his old round-shouldered stance, feet pointed inwards. He will be sucking his thumb next. Sasha keeps on crooning her Satanic lullaby until . . .

'Listen!' She screeches, a bloodcurdling sound that stops Rob in his tracks. His arms go limp at his sides and he is now staring straight ahead at nothing in particular. Unless the bastard is taunting us, she has just conducted a successful hypnotic induction. Maybe it's easier because he's listened to her through hundreds of hours of trance-type situations while restrained or hooded or . . . I don't know. Jung did it once just by shouting at someone, and stage hypnotists do it all the time, and I have the evidence of my eyes. Rob is standing stock-still on automatic pilot as he waits for her to tell him what to do, who to be.

'You are going to do what I say, Rob,' says Sasha quietly and firmly. 'What I am going to ask you to do will not harm you in any way. You are a good person who has been temporarily destroyed by the evil being who presently has you in its grip. You can make amends by helping us down from these crosses.'

He shuffles over and starts to work on the ropes binding Sasha's arms.

'Good boy!' she says, her tone of voice approximating that of a mother congratulating her three-year-old son for not wrecking the place for two consecutive minutes. He works slowly and methodically until she topples from the cross, her face screwed up in agony as she copes with the restoration of circulation and the impact of the fall. She tells him to untie me.

I can't start kicking him to death just yet though because I have to endure the same process Sasha's just been through, rolling around on the floor as my blood burns its way through my veins. When I can stand, Sasha hands me a coke.

'Don't hit him,' she says – seriously, as far as I can make out.

'What?'

'He has a lot of money. Don't you want any of it?'

I drain the coke in one then start throwing it up in as dignified a manner as I can manage. When I've finished crouching in front of a pile of fizzing blood-flecked vomit I stand up and grab the baseball bat he was going to use to break our legs.

'Don't!' she says, and just as greed wrenches me round to her point of view there are the sounds of a car outside.

I've had enough. I can't cope. This had better be the police, and I hope they have straitjackets because they just might need them. I grab Rob's gun, although I don't know where the safety is or if it's still loaded, and hobble up the stairs. I can see through the spyhole that it's Sasha's Papa, who actually looks his age for once, stooped and drawn, holding a hat that was fashionable about thirty years ago.

'What do you want?' I ask, opening the door.

'Is Sasha all right?' he says.

'I'm fine, Papa,' says Sasha, who has crept up the stairs without my noticing. I wish she wouldn't do that. 'How did you get here?'

For a moment it seems as if he is too weary to answer, but then he thinks better of it. 'I've been listening to everything that happens in your flat since last year,' he says. 'I bugged your house.' There is a nasty, triumphant smile on his face as he watches us cope with that. I feel sick again, but there are too many questions to ask.

'You left the messages on our answerphone,' I say.

He doesn't care. After a lifetime killing people, why should he?

'I didn't like her messing about with black magic,' he says in a flat, dull monotone that would seem to suggest he has had enough. Of everything.

'And you killed Nails,' says Sasha.

More weary silence. I don't think he's come to apologise.

'I cut off his dick so he wouldn't stick it in you. I only wish I could have cut his off as well,' he says, nodding at me. For some reason Sasha looks sympathetic.

'What's wrong, Papa? You look ill,' she says.

Not the approach I would have taken, but maybe she's channelled some Xtian forgiveness while we were up on the crosses. A flash of the old anger flickers behind Papa's eyes.

'What's wrong? Apart from cancer? I wanted a fine upstanding son. A soldier. We end up with you. Ah, well.'

It's probably supposed to be a joke, but he needs to work on his timing because Sasha's eyes harden. 'You always did this to me. You and her,' she says, almost choking with anger. 'You made me what I am!'

'I know. And now I'm dying, I just want to tell you you're better than this piece of shit.' He nods at me. 'You won't listen now but maybe you will later.'

She walks over and hugs him. He looks gloatingly over at me as he returns her embrace.

'We'll get you some help, Papa,' she says. 'It's not too late.'

'There's no cure for what I've got,' he says.

'You're right there, mate,' I say, to no one in particular.

'I just wanted to tell you how much I loved you. If you love me.'

'Of course I love you,' she sobs.

'. . . then ditch him.'

He pushes her away then reaches into the pocket of his anorak and produces a gun which he jams against his temple. 'Say you'll ditch him.'

'I won't. You can't make me! You always have to guilt-trip me!'

'We sacrificed everything for you and you become a whore. Why?'

'I'm not a whore! Sex is art. It's therapy. It's a healing process. I'm an artist . . .' – who sounds like it's a long time past her bedtime. Daddy does that chuckle of his.

'I could just shoot him anyway,' he says.

'No!' She screams and runs towards him. He manages to hug her tightly to him without relinquishing his grip on the gun.

'Daddy, don't.' She's weeping now as she repeats the phrase over and over again.

'I suppose you'll grow out of him. In time,' he says, as the tears die down. 'I just won't be there to see it.' That sets off a fresh flood of tears.

'There must be a cure. Don't give in, Daddy.'

'Look at me,' he says. She looks into his eyes. 'I want to see the face of an angel for the last time.'

'Don't do it! We'll get you help.' Her voice cracks at the hopelessness of it all as she pounds on his chest with both fists.

'I love you,' he says, gently pushing her out of range.

Sasha bunches her fists in frustration and screams at him.

'All right! Do it, then! See if I care.'

He blows her a kiss then pulls the trigger, spraying red and grey stuff up the nearest wall. When the screaming and the vomiting and the weeping stop we both have a medicinal brandy sat round the kitchen table while talking rubbish about the transience of human life, reincarnation and why Sasha shouldn't feel guilty about her risky gamble. We say this several times at different volumes like it isn't going to take another five incarnations to work that one off until we remember Rob.

'How long is that trance going to last?' I say, already starting to feel more concerned about how much brandy we have left.

'How should I know?' says Sasha, and she has looked better. 'He might be drifting out of it now.'

I hurtle down the stairs but he is still where we left him, staring at the floor, a long string of saliva hanging from his mouth.

'Are you going to wake the sleeping beauty?' I say when Sasha has joined me.

'You behave yourself,' she says. 'When I count to three you will wake up, Rob. You will feel no ill effects. One, two, three.'

He comes to with a dreamy smile, which fades as he sees us standing right next to him. All the old aggression reappears, then he draws a combat knife from a holster strapped to his ankle. He turns the blade on himself, placing the tip carefully between two ribs. 'Don't *you* start,' I say, but he's off, foaming at the mouth just as he was before the hypnotic interlude.

'You haven't won,' he says. 'I'll show you the Black Rite. I'm going to turn it on you!'

Just as I'm thinking, Be my guest, Sasha starts begging him not to do it. I can't see the percentage in that, but she has this irrational thing about preserving human life.

'I'm going to live inside your head for ever,' says Rob in his stage villain voice.

He looks at me. 'You won't be living with Sasha any more. You will be living with me. You won't be fucking her; you will be fucking me. You will spend eternity with me!'

Well, I hope you floss, crosses my mind, but he's putting a lot into this performance. And he's convinced Sasha.

'Don't do it!' She is sobbing now. She knows him better and she must be certain that he is going to use the knife in his hand.

'No!' screams Sasha, raising only the hint of a smile from Rob.

'I won't say goodbye because I'm going to be inside you,' he taunts. 'For ever!'

Sasha's scream coincides with the sight of Rob plunging the knife through his ribs. He takes a long time to die and it's horrible to look at, but I watch to make sure he's not planning another one of his comebacks. When he has twitched his last she has no more tears to shed. I look down at Rob's shell and feel absolutely nothing.

Something about how much product he is going to shift now

he's dead flashes through my mind, but I'm not jealous of his immortality. It's better being alive right now. And while she's off her guard there has never been a better time to ask a question that has been bothering me for years.

'You did Spider,' I say. She nods. I suppose I have always known.

'He wanted me to. He was in a lot of pain. He really didn't want to live.'

Which would have been an impressive argument if he had been fifty years older.

'So it was consensual then. That's your excuse for everything. Don't do me, will you?' I say.

'As if I would.'

Very reassuring. Sasha perks up considerably when she sees the Porsche.

'Cool!' she says.

'You're going to be thirty soon,' I say.

A playful three-fingered strike catches me on the septum. Now *that* hurts.

'Where did you learn to do that?' I say.

'You kept going on and on about those unrealistic film scenes where women throw punches without breaking their fingers,' she says happily.

'Yeah, yeah. You're not going to do any of that hypnotism stuff on me?' I say.

'I do it all the time. You just don't notice,' she says as she tunes the radio in to some depressed students and we drive off, leaving the bodies to rot.

I'm looking forward to seeing the neighbourhood's reaction to seeing us roll up in a genuine modern art masterpiece. Funny how I feel different about this car now it belongs to us. It doesn't exempt us from the uptown traffic, but we still feel pretty good driving through lower Manhattan. Then I notice the cluster of squad cars outside our house. Another work of modern art comes to mind: *The Electric Chair* by Andy Warhol. Is it going to be Sasha or me who gets to sit in it?

Maybe they'll do the two of us at once to save on the utility bills. We could drive on, I suppose, but we aren't going anywhere without money or passports.

'Is there a problem, officer?' says Sasha as she draws in to the curb.

A weary man with jowls like an elephant's arse wipes a beefy forearm over his sweating face. 'Guy shot himself on the third floor.'

I picture our upstairs neighbour, the thin sallow-faced Puerto Rican who always dressed in black. Kept himself to himself, as they say.

'Was it over a woman?' I ask, just to see if I can still speak after the near heart attack I have just suffered.

The cop chews some gum before deciding to elaborate. 'The guy was obsessed with black magic. He's got some sort of shrine up there. A real wacko. Hey – you're lucky he didn't put a hex on you.'

'You're right there,' I say, slumping back into the seat.

Sasha and I check the flat then decide we need to pack and then drive the Porsche somewhere, anywhere, away from here.

As soon as we are off, Sasha starts to sing 'Dancing on Delancey'.

'You see, he is living inside our heads,' I say. 'The Black Rite does work.'

'Don't even think that. Actually, what we need to close this deal is a baby. A new beginning.'

'Yeah, right. Can we cope with a foul-smelling bundle of incoherent rage? The incessant clamouring for attention . . .'

'I lived with you when you were drinking. Remember?'

'I don't, actually. We used to laugh more often, though.'

'And cry. All that self-pity. And the suicidal monologues, and the pointless violence and . . .'

'Yes, yes, we know all that . . .'

'And the smell of vomit, and the way you used to sweat. And swear all the time.'

'Change the record . . .'

'Change the record? I keep forgetting how old you are.'

We haven't had this one for a while. I must be winning. Surely not?

'I thought DJs used records in preference to CDs.'

'No one says what you just said. "Change the record".'

'He's going to be a boy,' I say, patting her abdomen. I'm trying to annoy her but it just makes bigger dimples pucker up and her eyes sparkle and . . . oh my. As we stop at the lights we share a kiss. A fat bag-lady eating a knish from a nearby stall snorts with disgust as we fold our arms around each other and get into some impressive tongue fu. It's hard to stop as it's been a while since the last one.

'Public displays of affection make me wanna barf,' she says, loudly and with a lot of feeling, but we are not going to stop just for her. When we unclinch there is enough sparkle left in Sasha's eyes to do it again, and then she just sits there giving me a wide dimple-flavoured smile that is simultaneously sweet, nourishing and a little cloying, perhaps, but deceptively strong. More or less like a bottled Guinness in a pint glass mixed with a barley wine and a double brandy. That's the effect it has, anyway.

'I'm addicted to you, babe,' I say.

'That's all right, my big grouchy bear,' she says happily. 'It's a co-dependency thing.'

As the lights change I look back to see if we managed to make the fat lady barf.